I0727384

Revolution of the Dead

OTHER BOOKS BY ANTHONY GIANGREGORIO

THE DEAD WATER SERIES

DEADWATER
DEADWATER: Expanded Edition
DEADRAIN
DEADCITY
DEADWAVE
DEAD HARVEST
DEAD UNION
DEAD VALLEY

ALSO BY THE AUTHOR

DEAD RECKONING: DAWNING OF THE DEAD
THE MONSTER UNDER THE BED
DEAD END: A ZOMBIE NOVEL
DEAD TALES: SHORT STORIES TO DIE FOR
DEAD MOURNING: A ZOMBIE HORROR STORY
ROAD KILL: A ZOMBIE TALE
DEADFREEZE
DEADFALL
DEADRAGE
SOUL-EATER
THE DARK
RISE OF THE DEAD
DARK PLACES

DEAD WORLDS: Undead Tales (Contributing story and editor)

Revolution of the Dead

Anthony Giangregorio

Revolution of the Dead

Copyright © 2009 by Anthony Giangregorio

ISBN   Softcover ISBN 13: 978-1-935458-17-3
                        ISBN 10: 1-935458-17-5

All rights reserved. No part of this book may be reproduced or transmitted in any form or by any means, electronic or mechanical, including photocopying, recording, or by any information storage and retrieval system, without permission in writing from the copyright owner.

This is a work of fiction. Names, characters, places and incidents either are the product of the author's imagination or are used fictitiously, and any resemblance to any actual persons, living or dead, events, or locales is entirely coincidental.

This book was printed in the United States of America.

For more info on obtaining additional copies of this book, contact:

www.livingdeadpress.com

Acknowledgments

Thanks to my wife, Jody, and son, Joseph, as always for helping me with this book, and to Marc and Adam for their advice and time.

AUTHOR'S NOTE

This book was self-edited, and though I tried my absolute best to correct all grammar mistakes; there may be a few here and there.
Please accept my sincerest apology for any errors you may find.

Visit my web site at undeadpress.com

Revolution begins with the misfits...

H.G. Wells

Chapter 1

Notes from Professor Cassius Richmond, PhD. June 2015

No one expected the plague to happen, who would?

Sure, everyday on the television was another report about bird flu or Sars or some mosquito carrying the bubonic plague, but no one ever expected the small microbe that killed nearly all human life on the small blue planet called Earth to come from the ocean. I mean, the ocean was always our friend. Sure, we dumped chemicals into it by the tons and spilled enough crude oil in it to run a thousand jet planes for a hundred years, and sure, we fished sections of it barren, but it was the ocean, for God's sake.

We came from it, crawled out of it and never looked back. We forgot where we came from.

But the ocean didn't.

Like some kind of maniacal mind, some form of evil genius, the ocean waited, bided its time until it felt it was time for revenge.

And that revenge came in the form of microscopic microbes released from an underground cavern when a survey expedition began drilling for more oil in the spring of 2010, one hundred miles off the Alaskan coast, broke through the ice and found death for us all.

Once released, the microbe infected every single ocean inhabitant. Every flounder, lobster and whale. Every bluefish, crab and starfish. Every tuna, shark and dolphin, every…Well, I think you get my meaning.

Now, that wouldn't have been so bad in and of itself as the microbe was not airborne, but you see, we eat almost every living creature in the ocean, like it is our God given right to devour anything that isn't as sentient as us. And if it is not our equal, then it doesn't have a right to exist, unless it is feeding, or in some way, serving us.

So we ate the ocean denizens. We devoured our baked shrimp with butter, the roasted lobster tails, and the clam chowder. We ate our tuna fish and the Japanese ate their whale, though they weren't supposed to, but that is another story. Where was I? Oh, yes, so we ate our shark steaks and swordfish and our crab cakes, and the entire time we did this, we were slowly killing ourselves; poisoning ourselves with these microbes.

The entire world found out that the mercury content of fish was the least of our worries. It didn't happen suddenly like in some science-fiction movie or an Italian horror flick. Instead, it began gradually. All over the globe people began getting sick. Like most diseases, it had viral symptoms. Coughing, sneezing, runny noses, that sort of stuff. Let me tell you, that was the time to own stock in Robitusin and Nyquil.

But soon after the first flu-like symptoms began, the hosts grew worse.

The second stage was similar to pneumonia. Once pneumonia set in, of course, the body was vulnerable to all kinds of diseases and bacterium.

Not that it mattered, however, because the microbe, later identified and labeled as The Blood Virus, was still working, digging deep into the cells of the suffering hosts.

In the last stage of the disease, the host lost more than half its blood, every orifice expelling the viscous fluid like it was a contaminant. There was no way to stop it. At first it would begin with a nose bleed, then the eyes and ears would seep blood, and finally nose and genital areas became nothing but crimson fountains.

With more than half the host's blood expunged, there was not enough oxygen to feed the brain and the heart withered and died, the victim falling into a deep coma before expiring.

People died by the millions, one at a time and in groups. Hospitals became nothing more than giant morgues, stacking the dead like cordwood. Massive graves were dug; bodies buried and burned by the thousands, but there were just simply too many corpses for any single population to handle.

And with each added death, there was one more body to destroy, and one less person to help the dead and dying.

Weeks turned into months, and then, on the fourth month, there was a slowing of deaths. Fewer and fewer of the population were expiring and it was soon realized the virus was either, a) running its course, or b) the remaining three percent of the population was immune to the microbe.

With only three percent of the population left alive, there was almost no one to run the world. And the decaying corpses of the dead were still everywhere, rotting and decomposing in piles. Every hospital was still packed with carcasses of dead people and no one wanted to go in there and clean up the massive amount of bodies. The smell alone was enough to make a garbage man cry.

So the world slammed to a halt as the few remaining survivors tried to get back on their feet. But it was nearly impossible to do all the things we once did, most of them practicalities and necessities.

A hundred and fifty years ago, each home was self-sufficient. They had wells for water and outhouses for defecating and gardens for vegetables. Farm animals were raised for eggs and meat. But that all changed in the early twentieth century. Things are so very different now.

Now we get our tomatoes from California, our broccoli from Georgia, our tobacco from Kentucky and our milk from Maine. We get our oranges from Florida and our bananas from Columbia and our wheat from Kansas and our potatoes from Ohio.

It's a very different world, even our water is pumped to us now from reservoirs and our feces is taken away to be processed and cleaned so it doesn't contaminate the land and water supply. There are people who do all that. If not, we'd all starve and be buried under our own human waste.

Case in point, the electrical plants. There was no one to run them as almost everyone who worked at each one across the world had perished from the virus.

Growing foods such as wheat and rye, and tomatoes and oranges, still went ahead, but with no one to harvest them, the crops soon rotted on the ground. The remaining survivors knew they could eat canned goods for a while, but they wouldn't last forever. Besides, they still wanted their internet, their Starbucks, their Baby Gap, and their Home Depots. No one wanted to revert back to the 1800's and ride bicycles and make their own clothing and grow their own food.

So a solution had to be done and fast so there were people to drill for oil, harvest the crops, and wash our cars, because the remaining people didn't want to do it and more than ninety-nine percent of Mexico was dead. No one was coming to America anymore, hell, some of us Americans went there instead. At least those who wanted to leave the old ways behind and live more simply.

We needed a work force, one that would do all the things the Spanish, the Mexicans, the El Salvadorians and others who had come to America for a better life and ended up scrubbing toilets, working deep fat fryers, and cutting our lawns for a living.

And that's where I came in. I was already working on a serum for bringing back victims of sudden and natural death. I wanted to pass the six minute window for the human brain and extend it to days, weeks and even months. My research was designed on the assumption that the human brain retains all that it is, like a hard drive does even after the computer has been turned off and unplugged. The trick was how to retrieve all that information after the computer was off and you had no power. I won't go into boring details about my failures, but I will tell you about my one triumph, though like many discoveries, this one was a direct result of me working on my serum.

It was during the first month of the plague that I had my first break through. I had so many subjects I was giggling like a school girl, I was as happy as a clam. So far my serum had been unresponsive, but then, during one of the trials, something amazing happened.

The corpse on the table actually moved a finger. At first no one saw it happen; and why would they? There were more than a dozen other researchers with me at the time, all moving about the lab, checking past notes and trying to see what serum A had in common with serum B. For the sake of the average minded person, I have tried to dumb it down here, not wanting to bog this tale down with fancy phonetics and medical jargon so the common man can understand what miracle had occurred right under my nose.

We had all been up for days and were quite exhausted, so no one saw movement from subject, 11-453. We were all desperate to find a cure for the Blood Virus, or Bloody V as it was called on the streets, that no one noticed the fruits of our labor until a scrub nurse dropped a tray on the ground, the racket like the firing of a starter gun at a marathon. All eyes turned to her and she gazed back at each of us. Then her eyes slowly moved down to the corpse on the table, the corpse that now had its eyes open and was looking around, its eyes darting back and forth like it was watching a tennis match.

I skip ahead so as not to bore you now, wanting to keep the story going forward.

After hundreds of tests we found out that by adding a certain level of the antivirus for Sars, the subject's brain finally kick-started.

But there was one very important problem that I could not overcome. Though I had managed the impossible by bringing the dead back to life, I had not overcome the six minute window. Unfortunately, for all purposes, the subject was still technically brain dead, but still seemed to have moderate motor function and basic instincts.

I laugh now as I say this, but one of my associates joked that it was a zombie and would try to eat our faces off, but we soon found the creature was benign. It was like a young child, staring at us with wonder and we soon found out it had basic learning skills.

It could be taught to perform the most basic functions, such as walking a dog and cutting the lawn, and other menial tasks that we as a civilization have always said a monkey could do and yet never did. There was another problem as well. It seemed the antivirus kicked started the brain, but not the rest of the internal organs. Somehow the brain was keeping the subject "alive", to use the term loosely. So though it moved and interacted with the world around it, its flesh was quite literally rotting off its bones.

Later, we found that embalming a subject didn't affect its reanimation and that helped quite a lot to keep the decomposing to a minimum. With frequent bacterial scrubs and a good coat of wax, your 'average zombie', if you'll let me use that word, though archaic, will last for years and years.

It wasn't long before my discovery was noticed by what was left of the military and soon a deal was brokered with a few private contractors that managed to remain functional during the central collapse of the world thanks to the Blood Virus. Within six months of my initial discovery, the first "zompal" was rolled off the assembly line to make the remaining three percent of humanity's lives easier.

It wasn't long before zompals were everywhere, delivering your milk, painting your house, driving your buses--with the help of a magnetic navigational system locked to a specific route that could not be deviated from--cutting your grass and unloading your food that was harvested by the zompals in another state.

With this undead workforce, the world got back on track. People prospered and the virus of Bloody V was forgotten, pushed to the back of the world's minds. It had always been so. No matter how terrible the tragedy, no matter how many have suffered, the world likes to forget, people like to forget. Maybe it's a coping mechanism, the human consciousness not wanting to deal with the dangers hanging over all of our heads like a giant guillotine.

Or maybe we're all just too stupid to exist and it would have been better if Bloody V had been stronger with a 100% mortality rate.

For five years after the Blood Virus wreaked its terrible vengeance on humanity, the world was a utopia. With so few existing where so many once lived, there was plenty of land, food and resources to go around. Gas and oil was less than a dollar a gallon as there was no one to use it like before.

The only real difference from the world of 2010 and now was that everywhere a person looked there were dead people walking around, acting like butlers from a Lon Chaney movie. Don't know who he is? Google him.

There was one more thing, actually. Technology stood still. With 99.9% of the great minds of the world dead or scooping your dog's poop with a bloated stomach and rotting flesh, there was no one to invent all the wonderful toys we as a people have enjoyed over the years. No more microwaves, no more new cars, no more waves of the future items on television. Time stood still. Though it was 2015, it was still 2010 to anyone still living, only less crowded.

One of my favorites was my commute to work every morning. What used to take an hour, now takes twelve minutes, as the amount of cars I see as I make my way can be counted in the single digits sometimes.

So if that was the end of my story, things probably wouldn't sound so bad, right? Well, at least if you're one of the survivors, and to tell you the truth, yeah, it was pretty sweet.

But then something happened, something no one would have foreseen in their worst nightmares.

The dead we used for cheap labor, the dead we used to run our errands and sweep our streets, the dead we used to paint our buildings and collect our trash, 'changed'.

How did they change, you may ask?

Well, they began to think for themselves, and the first thing they thought, with that first spark of intellect, was that they didn't like being our slaves.

And they were going to do something about it.

Chapter 2

Marsha Lambert closed her eyes and let the wind blow through her light blonde hair.

It was a beautiful sunny day, the kind that makes you glad you were alive. She felt guilty at thinking that, guilty about thinking that because the sun was out she should be grateful for being one of the 3% who had somehow managed to avoid being wiped out by the plague years ago.

But five years was a long time to think about *what ifs* and *what might have beens*. She was twenty-three now and the world was at her feet. The sprawling city flew by to her sides. Once mighty conglomerates, department stores and food chain outlets, would have greeted her gaze, but now there were long streets where nothing was open. Even after five years, there were still places where it looked like the plague had just occurred.

Sometimes for a lark, her friends would go there, digging through the dead of the past as if they were archeologists searching for that next big find, but she never did. She had been eighteen when Bloody V first hit and within three weeks of the first reported case her parents had both been in commas. Days later, they had died and Marsha had been left all alone in a vastly shrinking world. She was lucky though, her Aunt Nancy had taken her in. Nancy had lost loved ones, as well, including her mom and almost every single extended relative in their family.

Nancy was a widow now and she and Marsha had forged a bond in sorrow that not many could replicate.

On top of her parents, Marsha had also lost her fiancée. Seth had been her high school sweetheart and someone she could tell anything to. They had been only a month away from getting married when he had died. In many ways, his death was the worst loss of all, but she had remained strong, and with her Aunt's help, had managed to carry on, like so many others along with her.

"Hello? Earth to Marsha, come in Marsha," a voice said from the front seat of the two-door, red convertible she was riding in.

Marsha's eyes focused on the face gazing back at her and she shook her head.

"Did you want something, Chad?" Chad's eyes creased slightly and the corner of his mouth curled up into a leer. "Nope, just enjoying the view."

She followed his gaze to see he was staring at her legs, which were now exposed thanks to a particularly strong gust of wind which had swept through the interior of the car. Her strawberry-cream panties were visible, with just the slightest indentation where her upper thighs met her loins. She quickly pushed her dress back down.

Chad pouted, disappointed the exhibition of her shapely legs and panties were now closed for the day.

"Aww, you're no fun," he joked and turned back around.

With Chad facing forward in the passenger's seat, Marsha let a smirk cross her lips. Chad was such a hornball; he would screw anything that had a hole, animal, mineral or in-between. She stared at the back of his neck, his brown hair cut clean and tight, military style. The shape of his head was slightly square and his features were sharp, like he'd been carved out of stone with a hammer and chisel instead of born naturally like the rest of humanity. He was ruggedly handsome, with a casual charm that brought most women to their knees, Marsha included. He was tall and muscular with deep blue eyes and Marsha had a crush on him, though she would never, ever, tell him this. Chad would only use her and toss her away like he'd done to countless others, and though she sometimes wondered if it would be worth it, she didn't want to become just another notch on his belt.

Instead, she wanted to be Mrs. Chad Trenton one day.

Well, a girl could dream, couldn't she?

In the driver's seat was Robert Forester, his red hair slicked back and his collar up like a reject from a 1950's movie. He was James Dean reincarnated, if James Dean had sprouted red hair and freckles. His left hand was to his side, hanging over the lip of the driver's door with palm open, catching the breeze while he shot down the middle of Grand Avenue.

Leaning back in his seat, he glanced at Marsha.

"Hey, babe, I'm gonna get the car washed, you mind?"

Marsha shrugged. "No, fine with me, just as long as we get there by three."

Robert raised his right hand and made a wave with it, his way of saying *everything was under control.* "Not a problem, babe, you're with me, and I always have things under control."

Chad made a raspberry sound and let out a loud chortle. "Ha, are you serious?"

Robert glared at him, fire in his eyes. Well, maybe more like smoldering coals. Robert and Chad were always at odds, but Chad was usually the winner at whatever competition the two were embroiled in at the moment. Still, Marsha couldn't blame Robert for his will to win. Perhaps one day he would best Chad. She may have a silent crush on him, but she too, would welcome that day, as hopefully it would squelch his ever-growing ego just a little bit.

Robert slowed as he approached the carwash, getting in line behind a small Toyota. With less people living, there was less congestion, and for the survivors that had its perks. No more waiting at the registry for hours or running into the post office to mail a letter to wait twenty minutes.

America was a much quieter place with less people in it, though there could also be disadvantages, too.

Because all the hired help was dead, or maybe undead was a better description.

Robert slowed and waited his turn, watching the car attendant taking money from the Toyota and then scratching something on the windshield with a piece of washable chalk. The attendant had a baseball cap on, and he couldn't see the man's face very clearly. Tired of waiting even thirty seconds, he began fiddling with the radio and then the top for the car, having to close the roof so he could wash the vehicle.

The Toyota moved forward and then the attendant was waving him on in slow, jerky gestures.

Chad slapped Robert on the arm, seeing the attendant waving them forward.

"Hey, idiot, the guy says you can go," Chad told him with a smirk.

Robert looked up from the radio, though trying to find a station, and glanced to Chad, a frown on his lips.

"I know, jerk wad, give me a sec'."

Ignoring the radio, Robert drove forward, slowing when he reached the man.

"What do ya need, pal?" The man asked lazily. He was bored with his job, but only a human could do it. The dead had their uses, but they couldn't think.

"Give me the regular, any specials today?" Robert inquired.

The man took Robert's money while shaking his head.

"Nah, only the works got a special. Three bucks off, you want it?"

Robert weighed the thought, but decided against it.

"No, I'm good, regular will do for today."

The man nodded, counted off the change from the money Robert had handed him, and gave it back. Robert took it, made it disappear and with a grin, glanced to Marsha.

"I'll use what I didn't spend on the car for lunch," he told her.

"Thanks, Robert, that's mighty nice of you," she replied.

Chad grunted, annoyed that on this one subject he wouldn't be able to get the upper hand.

Robert was a trust fund kid. When his parents had died from the plague, he had inherited everything they had, which was quite substantial. He was set for life and he knew it.

He wasn't a jerk about it, but to Chad it was a sore spot as he was just scraping by, his family barely middle-class.

Robert was waved forward and he began to drive until his left front wheel hit the runner that would steer the car through the carwash.

The top was down and they all relaxed while the water spray began washing the car clean of dirt.

No one spoke, each of them staring out the window as the water sluiced off the roof, the cloth rollers slapping the glass like soft, tiny hands.

When the car had reached the end, ten bodies surrounded it, their damp rags already prepared to begin wiping whatever water remained on the vehicle.

Rob leaned back and let the helpers go to work, but as he watched, his grin quickly turned into a frown as he realized what was happening.

"Hey, what the hell? Aww, come on, I just drove it out for Christ's sake!"

Chad began to chuckle as he watched a decrepit ghoul making a mess of Rob's hood, leaving streaks of dark brown blood and clear and yellow pus across the finish.

At first Marsha didn't know what was happening, but then another carwash ghoul moved to her side window and began wiping the dirty rag across the glass. Unfortunately, there was more blood than water in the rag and it left slime streaks all over the window.

"Oh, that's so gross," she said as she watched the dead face, the eyes blank and devoid of emotion.

"Hey, man, get away from my car! Get off!" Robert yelled as he opened his door, knocking two ghouls to the ground. The zombies lay sprawled on the ground like turtles, not fully understanding why they were now horizontal. In his anger, Robert took it out on the closest ghoul, his foot swinging out to connect with the forehead of it. His steel tipped boot collided with the skull of the ghoul and sank three inches into the brittle flesh and bone.

"Oh, great, now I ruined my shoe shine, too!" Robert screamed pulling his boot back as tendrils of gristle clung like a toddler's saliva.

"Hey, hey, what the hell do you think you're doing?"

Robert turned to see the man he'd given his money to running at him, waving his hands in the air. Behind the man, cars honked; annoyed they had to wait to be served.

"Hey, Robert, maybe you should give it a rest," Chad said from the car. He didn't want to get into any trouble, which was the way the situation was going. On the ground, the ghoul with a large dent in its head flailed around, like a few wires in its already numb brain had been crossed.

Robert turned on the owner of the carwash, anger in his eyes.

"What am I doing? Jesus, pal, just look at my car? These deadheads ruined the finish?" While he was yelling, the other zombies continued wiping their filthy rags across the car, the slime trail of yellow and red dripping down the panels to pool on the ground. Marsha had to wonder where they got all those bodily fluids if they were dead.

"Well, you didn't have to beat up the help, shit, buddy, just drive it around and go through again, on the house."

"Damn straight it's on the house," Rob said. He turned to the ghoul on the ground and kicked it again, a few ribs cracking, the sound like brittle branches being snapped.

"Hey, quit it! I said you could go through again. You want me to call the cops?"

"Come on, Robert, give it a rest already," Chad called. "Just go through again so we can get out of here."

Robert turned to Chad, and though he was still mad, realized his friend was right. Turning, he walked back to his car.

"Fine, we'll go through again, but I'm not waiting in line again."

"No, of course not, just go around and I'll get you right in," the owner said. "Oh, shit, look what you did to this one, he's ruined! I can't use him with his head looking like that.

Robert climbed in the car and closed the door.

"Why, I think it's an improvement," he sneered.

"Robert, that's not nice, that was a human being at one time," Marsha said like an angry mother.

"Yeah, well, now it's a deadhead, so there." As if the matter was settled, he drove around and then honked at the entrance to the carwash, a few patrons upset he was cutting in line.

The carwash owner ran back around and let him in using the other lane which had been closed. After he removed the cones and Robert pulled in, he dropped them back down again, closing the lane once more.

A few angry questions were tossed at the owner, but he waved to the patrons, asking them to be patient and he would give them a discount for their aggravation.

The owner let Robert through and the car went into the wash yet again, only this time, at the exit, Robert made sure to steer clear of the ghoul attendants. As he drove out of the carwash, the ghoul he'd kicked was still on the ground, so sliding the wheel to the left, he made sure the tire lined up with the zombie's legs.

There was a slight bump when the car drove over the limbs and a loud crack filled the air, then the car was in the street and on its way.

Marsha glanced over her shoulder to see the ghoul floundering on the ground, its calves and feet now separated from the rest of it. The ghoul flailed around, not understanding what had happened to it and Marsha looked away, not wanting to see anymore.

"Oh, man, that ain't right," Chad said just after Robert had driven over the animated corpse.

"No, it isn't, how could you do that?" Marsha asked in a disapproving tone.

Robert heard none of it.

"Relax, Marsha, it's going to the dump anyway. The carwash owner said it himself."

Well, still, that was awful," she admonished him.

"Look, I'll say I'm sorry if it'll make you feel any better, okay? I'm sorry."

"No, you're not, you're just saying that," she replied, crossings her arms over her chest.

Rob grinned, glancing at her in the rearview mirror. She could only see his eyes, but she didn't like what was there.

"Yeah, you're right, I am, now let's put it behind us and go get some lunch."

Marsha glared at him, well, his eyes anyway, for three more seconds, and then she turned away.

Robert chuckled, and with his car now nice and clean, they drove down the empty road, their next stop lunch.

Chapter 3

As Robert drove deeper into the city, signs of life became more prevalent, and the ubiquitous number of zombies began to grow in size.

While the car sped down the street, Marsha glanced at the ghouls working and moving about on errands. Only the smartest ghouls were able to do even the most basic task and they had to be taught like dogs for weeks at a time until they finally learned things such as taking out the trash or walking a dog.

Marsha glanced to her right and saw one such ghoul doing just that. The dog was rather larger compared to the zombie, and as Marsha watched, the dog spotted an alley cat and took off in chase. The ghoul raised its arm, the hand holding the dog chain, but when the dog reached the limit of the chain, the arm popped off like a rotten twig. As the dog shot down the sidewalk, the rotting arm jumped and bounced behind it. She had just enough time to see the ghoul begin a chase and then the car was past.

More zombies appeared, one trying to scrub graffiti from a brick wall, another picking up trash. It took her a second to realize the car was pulling over and that Robert and Chad were talking excitedly.

"Let's fuck the deadhead up," Robert was saying, Chad laughing and nodding merrily.

Marsha glanced to where the two men were looking and she realized what was going to happen.

This wouldn't be the first time nor did she think it would be the last.

The car jolted to a halt and the two men jumped out,

"Come on, Marsha, aren't you gonna join us?" Robert asked.

She frowned deeply.

"Don't ask me to join in your antics, Robert. It's cruel and you know it," she replied brusquely, folding her arms across her chest.

"Cruel? Why, they're dead, Marsha, it's not like they can feel pain," he waved a dismissive hand to her and turned away. "Ah, forget it, you just won't listen."

"Then why do it, Robert? Why even bother them at all?" She asked pleadingly, hoping he would come to his senses.

He shrugged. "'Cause it's fun."

He went to join Chad who was already standing in front of the zombie, who had ceased picking up trash, not sure what to do with a person standing in front of it.

The ghoul wore the standard gray jumpsuit every undead city worker was made to wear with the exception of privately owned ones.

The body was decomposing and slumped forward, the shoulders sagging like an out of work man on his last dime. The mottled gray flesh was torn and pockmarked from exposure to the weather and bone peeked through here and there. Its hair was thin, falling out in numerous places, and a light beard was on its jaw, residual leftovers from when the skin had shrunk and grown tight on the skull, exposing the follicles already there beneath the surface of the flesh. What was amusing is, it looked like the ghoul was growing a beard and mustache, which would be ridiculous.

Robert and Chad ran up to the zombie and Robert reached out and slapped the cap off its head. The ghoul did nothing, merely stared at the two men with apathy.

Chad reached out and grabbed the green trash bag in its hand, then dumped the trash out to spread across the sidewalk. To make sure the trash was fully separated, he kicked it with his sneakers, the debris rolling and bouncing away.

"Ha, now its got to pick all this shit up again!" Chad yelled, loving every second of his actions.

"Stop it, both of you, you're just being mean," Marsha snapped from the back seat. She had begun looking around, hoping a police car might drive by. That would serve the jerks right. Messing with the undead workers was only a misdemeanor, but still, it would teach them a lesson.

"Oh, come on, Marsha, we're just having fun, lighten up a bit," Chad said.

"No, I will not, now if you two don't get back in this car right now I'm leaving, I'll walk home."

Robert sneered. "No, you won't, you live like ten miles from here, that's a lot of walking."

Marsha creased her eyes in anger as she stared Robert down.

"Just try me," she said.

Robert knew he didn't want her to walk; he liked her and was hoping one of these days they could be more than just friends.

So with a sigh, he pushed the ghoul so it stumbled away and then turned back to the car "Stupid deadhead," he mumbled as if it was the zombie's fault Marsha was now mad at him.

Chad was still kicking trash around and Robert called out to him.

"Come on, Chad, let's go, Marsha here doesn't like it."

Chad kicked one last crushed water bottle away from the ghoul, and then with a shoulder punch to the zombie's left side, he headed for the car.

The ghoul stared after the two men, its visage still slack, eyes watching impassively. The second Chad was gone; the ghoul began picking up the trash again, its treacle-like movements mimicking a tortoise.

*   *   *

The ride to the fast food restaurant was in silence, Marsha's steely, disapproving gaze keeping Robert and Chad from wanting to share in their debasement of the ghoul. They didn't understand what the big deal was. The thing was dead, it didn't feel emotions anymore, and if Robert wanted to get out some pent up aggression by smacking the ghoul around then what did it hurt?

The large M on the front of the restaurant was as obvious to them as their own names. When the world had crashed from the plague, only McDonalds had been able to survive, and that was because they were the only fast food chain to adopt the zombies as hired help. Where once Spanish and Mexican employees would have been frying the burgers and making the French fries, the entire design behind the counter was retooled so that the brain dead ghouls could now make the food. It wasn't much of a change from before.

There were many people who found this disgusting, but there weren't enough people to work in the restaurants anymore. And it was either this or the chain would close down, like the hundreds of others before it, most people accepting it as better than nothing.

Chad, Robert and Marsha entered the restaurant and were immediately stopped in the tracks by a ghoul wearing a bright yellow polo shirt and a baseball cap with a big M on it. It had a broom and small bucket, its job to sweep the floors.

"Outta the way, deadhead," Robert said and shoved the body away from him. The ghoul stumbled away, but didn't act different or offended in any way, but went back to work. And why should it? After all, it was dead.

"You guys go sit down," Robert said. "I'll get us a couple of value meals." Without waiting for a reply, he went to the counter, while Chad and Marsha went to grab a table. The place wasn't crowded and wouldn't be for more than a generation as the population slowly began to grow again.

The only other human in the place was the man behind the cash register. While the zombies had been trained to cook and clean, they weren't intelligent enough to handle the money. Robert quickly ordered the food and a few minutes later was carrying a tray loaded with burgers, fries and shakes.

When he set it down on the table, they dug in.

"Cool, man, I'm starving," Chad said as he shoved French fries into his mouth while unwrapping a burger.

Marsha said nothing, still angry at the two men for acting so cruel to the zombie worker.

It was while Chad was shoving another handful of fries into his face, his mouth opening to stick them in, that Marsha cried out in alarm, stopping him cold.

"What, what's wrong, why'd you yell?" Chad asked, looking around for the problem.

Marsha put on a disgusted face and pointed to the French fries in his hand.

"Look at your fries," she said. "Oh, that's so gross."

"Oh, wow, man, there's a finger in your fries," Robert exclaimed as he realized what Marsha had seen. "Now that's what I call finger food," he joked as he began to laugh. Marsha didn't think it was funny at all, and felt sick.

Chad set the fries down, and sure enough, one index finger, now a dark brown from being cooked with the fries, was entwined with the food.

He pushed it to the side, the fingernail of the cooked digit falling off as he did so, and then without hesitation, he picked up the fries and shoved them in his mouth as if it was no big deal.

"Dude, what's up with that?" Robert asked.

Chad chewed happily, then after he had swallowed a little of his food, he shrugged.

"Hey, man, it's the price for having deadheads cook and clean for us. It's either get a finger in the fries once in a while or I'll be cooking the food and cleaning the streets myself, right? 'Sides, the high temp' of fryer oil would kill any germs in the finger."

Robert gave the man's words some thought, and after a moment, he nodded, his face taking on an enlightened look.

"Well, goddammit if you don't come up with some smart shit once in a while, Chad. That's very intuitive."

"Thanks. Hey, dare me to eat the finger, too?"

Marsha looked ill. "Oh, God, Chad, don't you dare. If you do, so help me I'll never talk to you again," she breathed.

"Okay, relax, I was just joking." Chad said with a slight smile. "Maybe."

"Dude, you are so sick," Robert said as he took a bite of his burger.

Chad grinned from ear to ear and shoved half his burger into his mouth, meat and bread sliding out in a brown slurry as he made a pig of himself.

"Oh, well, so much for manners," Robert said as Chad made an ass of himself. Robert turned to Marsha, a smirk on his lips as he watched Chad in his peripheral vision. "Hey, you want to go to the movie theater after we eat? They're playing back to back Rocky movies."

"Sure, why not," Marsha said, not having anything else to do. Besides she liked Stallone. It's a shame he was wiped out with the other ninety-nine percent of Hollywood. Even after five years there was still no Hollywood, and it would be years before new movies would be made.

Well, that is unless you wanted to make a zombie movie, then there were all the extras you could ever want just walking around, as they were cutting your grass and washing your car on a daily basis.

Chad shoved more food into his mouth, making baby noises at the same time. Robert laughed at his antics while Marsha rolled her eyes and dropped her burger onto the table, her appetite now gone, and wondered for the thousandth's time just why she hung around with these two idiots.

Chapter 4

Roger Shanlon entered his home, a heavy sigh escaping his lips. It had been a long day and he was exhausted.

The aroma of supper filled his senses and caused him to swallow a mouthful of saliva as he hung his jacket on the coat rack and walked through the hallway.

On both sides of him were pictures of lost loved ones, family and friends who hadn't been immune to the virus.

But by a miracle, he and his wife had survived, though they had lost their ten year old son, Andrew. He paused at the end of the hallway, as he usually did to stare at the smiling face of his lost son.

Andrew was always smiling, Roger thought. The boy had never been sad a day in his life and hadn't had a bad bone in his body. He had been a doer and Roger had no doubt the boy would have grown into a great man someday.

Of course now that was all in the wind, only empty dreams that could never be fulfilled. But where there was life there was hope and he and his wife, Tammy, had already begun trying again for another child. With luck she would be pregnant before the end of the year.

The acting President had bid every American citizen to get back on the horse and procreate. They needed to rebuild America and they needed children to do so.

Turning from the picture, he entered the main living area of his home. It was a wide open area, with a large fireplace to the right and a massive bookcase full of books from every decade all the way back to Shakespeare's plays. He had always been an avid collector and with things the way they were, many people besides himself had fallen back to old habits such as reading and taking walks with loved ones.

As he entered the room, he could see his wife at the opposite end. She was working in the kitchen and he smiled as he watched her work, as she wasn't aware he had arrived home yet.

He decided to surprise her, so sneaking up on her, he reached out and goosed her on the bum. But he didn't see she had a roasting pan in her hands and when he goosed her, she jumped, the roast in the pan jumping into the air to land on the floor, lolling to the side like a severed head as bits of juice seeped out of the meat like blood from a cracked skull.

"Oh my gosh! Roger, it's you, you scared me half to death!" She screamed and then knowing she was safe, glanced down sadly at the roast.

"Now, look what you did. The roast is ruined."

Roger scooped her up in his arms. "Nah, it's fine, just wash it off and throw some salt and pepper on it, I'll eat it," he nibbled her ear playfully. "Besides, I can start eating right now and have the roast later."

"Oh, for the love of God, you just got home. Go get cleaned up and I'll fix this mess you made me make."

He nodded, kissed her one last time on the cheek and moved away, but before he was ten steps, Tammy paused to call him back.

"Yes, my love?" He asked sweetly.

"It's about Jonah, Roger. He's been acting funny lately. He was supposed to rake the leaves and then take out the trash, but he hasn't done any of it," she said, her voice sounding scared.

"So why didn't you make him do it, Tammy? That's what the cattle prod is for," Roger replied testily. This always happened. He got the zombie to make things easier around the house and he still had to deal with the shit when he got home.

"Yes, I know that," she said, "but it's just...well, I hate using that thing, it seems so barbaric."

Roger sighed wearily. "No, it's not, Tammy, my love. They're dead, they don't feel pain like you or me."

"But how do you know that? He looks human, he has a name. Maybe he still feels pain."

"Dammit, no, he doesn't," he said with a cut of his hand like he was chopping wood with it. "Now, I don't want to keep talking about this over and over again. Its got a name so we don't have to call it an *it* or a *thing* all the time. Look, get the roast fixed and I'll take care of Jonah. Where is he? Still in the yard?"

"Yes, dear, he is. He hasn't moved for hours, he just keeps staring at something in that big oak tree in the corner."

"Fine, I'll be back in a few minutes," he said, his playful mood gone, now all business again.

She nodded and he turned away from her, crossing the living area and reaching the door that would lead to the backyard.

Hanging on the wall by the door was a cattle prod, the pointed tip looking wicked and out of place in the contemporary setting of the home. Roger took it down and opened the door. With one last glance to his wife, pleased to see she was dealing with the dropped roast, he headed out to deal with his no-good zombie.

When he was through with the dead bastard, the ghoul called Jonah would never disobey him again.

*   *   *

The ghoul named Jonah (thanks to the man who'd been issuing names that day feeling slightly religious) had been standing in the yard for hours, oblivious to his coming fate.

His skin was tight against his face and conformed to the bone like dried parchment. He wore the standard grey coveralls of most zombies and he had a collar around his neck for when he was chained up at night. Though the ghouls were as ubiquitous as ants or flies nowadays, and most humans had become dependent on them, most still felt safer if they were locked up at night; chained to the wall like dogs.

Jonah's hair was still black, slicked back to at least look neat. He had a distinguishing mark on his hair however, a shock of his hair on the left side of his scalp was white, similar to that of a skunk, only thinner. When he had been human he'd been teased about it, but he had always liked the patch of white, believing it gave him a look of independence. When he had been alive, he had been a willful soul and had worn the white stripe with honor. His father had also had one and it had always been something the two of them shared. Not to mention his girlfriend had always liked it, as well.

Jonah's eyes were milky white, and he looked like he had the worse case of cataracts in history. But still he could see, and at the moment he was staring at a small birds nest a few feet above him. In the nest, a family of blue jays chirped happily, the mother feeding the newly hatched babies.

Jonah didn't know why he was so enthralled by this scene of nature, but he was so focused on it he never heard Roger when the man exited the house and strolled towards him, the cattle prod in his hand.

Jonah didn't know or understand the dim memory he had of sitting on his grandfather's lap and looking at a large book filled with all kinds of birds in it. Back when he had been human, before the plague, he'd had memories and a life. He had countless memories of spending time with his grandparents on the weekend, both of them avid birdwatchers. Then he would enjoy hours of sipping lemonade, eating chocolate chip cookies, and talking with them on the front porch of their house in the country.

This memory was so far down inside his dead brain it would never come to fruition, but would always remain trapped in the place between life and death.

Or it would have if not for Roger's fatal mistakes that would be called a miracle in medical science.

"Jonah, wake up, you stupid bastard!" Roger called as he exited the house.

Jonah ignored him.

Roger was aggravated as he crossed the backyard, leaves getting kicked into the air by his shoes; he felt like screaming. There was a small bucket of water to the side of the yard, used for watering the flowers, and he picked it up, deciding to see if he could get the damn zombie's attention with it.

Crossing the remaining feet between himself and Jonah, he tossed the bucket of water onto the ghoul, immediately soaking Jonah from head to waist.

"Jonah, you dumb bastard, pay attention to me," Roger yelled, but Jonah heard nothing, his dead eyes only for the birds.

It was like he was in a trance.

"Fine, I tried to be nice," Roger said and raised the cattle prod to chest level. He jammed it into Jonah's side and electricity shot out, causing Jonah to twitch. The odor of burnt meat filled the yard, but still Jonah remained unresponsive. As a zombie, his tolerance for pain was ridiculously high. What would cause a living human to run screaming in pain was but a mere pinprick to the ghoul.

Jonah still ignored Roger, wanting to stare at the birds nest forever.

Tammy had come to the back door and she was calling out to Roger, not wanting him to make a scene.

"Go back in the house, honey, I'll take care of this and I'll be in soon," he told her, but she didn't listen, now getting worried.

Roger jabbed the cattle prod into Jonah's side again and an electrical arc filled Jonah's insides, a small amount of smoke appearing around the cattle prod's tips. But still Jonah ignored Roger.

"That's it, I'm gonna fix you good, you stupid fuck, then I'll see you're sent to the dump," he muttered as he raised the prod higher and jabbed the tip against Jonah's left ear. When he squeezed the trigger to the prod, electrical energy shot out, seeping into Jonah's dead brain. Then it stopped when Roger pulled it back. The prod was on its lowest setting and it wasn't having any effect at all.

"What?" Roger asked Tammy. She was yelling at him again, but he hadn't heard her.

"I said you can't do that to him," she said. "The man who delivered him said to never use the cattle prod on the head. It's the brain that keeps them going and if you fry that he'll stop working. And it's not covered under the warranty."

"Well, he's not working now so what the hell do I have to lose?" Roger snapped back, then with a dismissive wave to his wife, he turned back around to Jonah, who was exactly where he had been.

"Fine," Roger said as he turned the dial to maximum on the cattle prod. "Let's see how you like high. I'll fry that brain to pudding and get myself a new one. One that works when I tell it to."

Roger raised the cattle prod and jammed it against Jonah's head, squeezing the trigger and sending deadly volts into his brain. But where normally the current would have fried his brain like an egg on a skillet, there was something added to the mix this time.

Thanks to Roger tossing water on Jonah, his scalp was now dripping wet, and the added water helped to send the current around his head and into his torso. His brain got juiced, but not enough to destroy him, in fact it began to jump start synapses and rebuild corrupted nerve points and reawaken memories long forgotten.

Jonah's head twitched like it was on fire and he dropped to the grass, his arms and legs spasming. Roger gazed down at the jumping ghoul and laughed, kicking him in the ribs for good measure.

"Take that, ya stupid deadhead," Roger spit as he laughed at the misfortune of his slave. What did he care? He could get another one tomorrow and he would.

"Roger, no, what did you do?" Tammy called out, her hand over her mouth in distaste.

"I did what I had to do. If the damn thing won't work then it's no good to us. Don't worry, honey. I'll get another one tomorrow."

Jonah had stopped spasming and he sat up slowly, his eyes seeing things differently now. The images his brain processed weren't just befuddled blocks now, his mind, though still dulled, seemed to be able to apply names to the things he saw.

Roger stared down at his zombie, shocked to see it was still alive, so to speak.

"Damn it, looks like you're tougher than you look, buddy. That's okay, I can fix that," Roger said and moved closer with the cattle prod, the tips arcing current like a transformer struck by lightning. Jonah gazed up at Roger, and though he didn't understand what was happening, something deep, deep inside him woke up.

The instinct for survival.

When Roger was in reach of his pale hands, and preparing to jab the cattle prod against his head again, Jonah took both hands and grabbed Roger around his wrists, yanking the man to the grass and on top of him.

"What the fuck?" Roger gasped as he tried to get away from the ghoul. He wasn't scared, and why should he be? This creature that was once human was docile and would obey him. If he told it to walk off a cliff or jump off a bridge the ghoul would do so without complaint. He was the master and his will would be obeyed or there would be consequences, that was how it had been for five years and it would be that way for another five, probably longer. He was trying to get the cattle prod around and he managed to twist it and jab it into Jonah's side. Electricity crackled and Jonah winced. He wasn't in true pain, but he felt something he hadn't felt since dying. He knew the current wasn't good for him and now realized he needed to protect himself.

So with nothing but hands and teeth as weapons, he grabbed Roger by the head and leaned in, his teeth sinking into his master's flesh and tearing out his jugular.

Warm plasma shot into Jonah's mouth, and before he could stop himself, he began to swallow the hot plasma, along with chunks of Roger's flesh. Immediately he felt revived, and as if on instinct, like a starving man wanting to feed, he leaned in and began slurping at the blood; then when the fountain slowed he began to rip the skin and tissue, swallowing it whole as he went back for more.

Roger's face went a pale white as his life's blood drained out of him. His eyes rolled up into his head and his legs danced a jig on the grass, his heels digging furrows into the sod.

Tammy screamed, realizing what was happening, but not fully understanding and she dashed across the lawn to her husband's aid.

She dropped down next to him and cradled his head in her arms, her eyes wide as she stared at the blood-covered face of Jonah.

"I'll see you cut up into little pieces for this, you bastard," Tammy screamed as she realized Jonah had somehow attacked her husband.

Jonah processed those words and realized Tammy was a threat, as well. Though she had never raised a hand to him or used the cattle prod, she had watched passively while Roger did just that.

He hesitated for a moment as he stared at the crying woman, images of his grandmother coming back to him. He saw her face in his mind, smiling as she handed him a cookie, but then the image was gone and only Tammy's screaming face was there.

Jonah shook off whatever piece of humanity he had recovered, and before Tammy could get away or yell out, Jonah lunged for her, forcing her to the grass with him on top. Like a bizarre make-out session, he leaned down and gave her a hickey, but as he pulled away, a large gash in her throat pumped her blood onto the grass, the sod soaking it up like a sponge. Jonah dove in again and drank his fill, sucking at the neck wound like a baby to a teat.

Tammy gasped in surprise, and her mouth flopped open and closed as she slowly died. Her eyes fluttered and her left hand reached to the sky, as if she was hailing a cab for Heaven. Then it dropped to the grass, limp, and she closed her eyes. Jonah didn't see this as he was still feeding on her. His body felt full of energy and the sloth-like feeling he'd had since becoming a ghoul was gone.

He pushed off the dead woman and stood up, glaring down at his former masters. Memories flooded his brain as neurons fired and he began to remember who he once was.

His former name or where he had lived wasn't what he remembered.

What he remembered was he was a person, with rights and liberties that had been taken away from him as a zombie.

He turned to see others like him in the nearby yards and he realized he had been unobserved by any other humans.

It was still early in the day and the other families of the neighboring homes were still inside, only the zombie workers in the yards, as they tended to grass and weeding. To his left was a zombie pushing a lawnmower, the loud whine of it more than enough to drown out the screams of Tammy and Roger.

He tried to speak, his mouth opening and closing, but nothing came out but grunts and moans. His vocal cords had almost completely rotted away years ago, the delicate membranes now shrunken and withered, so he couldn't speak; plus, his tongue was shriveled and dry, lying there like a dead slug was in his mouth.

A small spark of imagination filled his mind and he leaned down and picked up the cattle prod, then began licking his fingers of the blood coating them. He realized in his now working brain that it was the cattle prod that had awoken in his intelligence. Squeezing the trigger, he watched the electricity arc back and fourth between the two contact points, the small spark reflecting the whites of his eyes.

An idea came to him as he enjoyed his newfound freedom to think for himself and he crossed the yard, and stepped over the knee-high hedges separating the property, and when he was next to the ghoul cutting the grass, he stopped it. The ghoul did as it was told, following orders no matter who told it to.

Jonah looked around the yard and saw a small birdbath. Directing the ghoul to the birdbath, he took its head and forced it into the water. When the head and hair was good and wet, he yanked the ghoul up, and without preamble stuck the cattle prod against its temple and squeezed the trigger. Current filled the new ghoul's brain and the body fell to the grass, twitching, its eyes closed in what appeared to be pain.

A small tuft of smoke actually appeared to drift out of its ears and Jonah wondered if he had used too much current. But then the ghoul's eyes fluttered open and it looked around with a new intelligence that had been lacking only a few minutes before.

Jonah leaned down and helped the ghoul up. The new ghoul blinked, cocking its head in curiosity.

Jonah used his hands to try and explain what had happened and the ghoul nodded. This one could not speak either and whether it was a side effect of the current or his vocal cords were decayed as well didn't matter.

When the ghoul was caught up to speed, which took longer than it should have as it appeared this ghoul wasn't as intelligent as Jonah, they moved on. Only time would tell if this would be the case with all the ghoul's intelligence, but he would see soon enough.

Jonah directed his new ally to follow him. There were many, many yards filled with other zombies that needed to be brought into the fold and he would need all the help he could get.

The humans of the city didn't know it yet, but the balance of power in the world was about to change. The zombies had been the slaves for long enough. It was time they took back what was rightfully theirs. They outnumbered the humans twenty to one and soon they would be strong enough.

As Jonah led the new ghoul to the next back yard, his white eyes glittered with something more than intelligence. They now shone with an emotion that was very, very human.

They were now filled with vengeance.

Chapter 5

Whether there are a million people, or just ten, in the world, there will always be some that are bad, or morally bankrupt in any civilization. No matter how lucky some might feel for surviving the plague, there will always be others who will squander the gift of life they were given.

Such was what was happening three blocks away from where Jonah was beginning to recruit his dead brothers and sisters to his cause.

The Broadway Bank was a small, one-story brick building with three teller windows and a small vault. It was a satellite branch, one once put in its location for the convenience of the customer than for any true need for it. Actually, before the plague hit five years ago, the branch was about to be closed, the bank wanting to downsize a little. But when the main part of the city became nothing but death and decay, the satellite branch had become indispensable for the bank to continue operating in and around the city.

Even now, five years later, the branch had become the actual headquarters for the bank, as most people didn't want to enter the actual city anymore. Even after five years and hundreds upon hundreds of cleanups by sanitation workers wearing haz-mat suits and bio filters, there were still buildings and apartments where the dead and rotting corpses still remained. Someday they would all be found, and when the population continued to grow, the city and others like it would become inhabited again. But for now, the massive, empty steel and stone buildings were a monument to another time, when man was everywhere and not confined to smaller towns across the globe.

The bank was being robbed, but the holdup had gone terribly wrong, one of the tellers pressing the silent alarm, and in less than four minutes, the first squad car arrived, followed by six more. This was the entire police force, the rest occupied by volunteers, much like the fire department. In a world where most of the experienced jobs were unoccupied, everyone had to lend a hand to keep things moving.

If a zombie could fight a fire or police the streets, no doubt they would have been trained to, but some things only a human being could do, their reasoning skills the deciding factor.

But that was not to say zombies could not still have their uses, such as what was happening now at the bank as a SWAT truck pulled up and began offloading its cargo.

A dozen ghouls, all tied together, were herded out of the truck to stand in the road. All wore the standard gray coveralls with one exception. These ghouls all had on SWAT baseball caps to identify them as part of the team, so to speak.

But that was where the similarity ended.

The four SWAT officers herded the zombies to the stone steps of the bank and then had to duck behind a car when shots rang out from the building. A side window was now broken, and a machine gun barrel pointing out to spray the area with lead slugs.

The police returned fire and the bank robber ducked back inside, pleased he still had dominance over the situation.

There would be no negotiating.

With a new world with less people in it came new laws. To rob a bank and threaten the lives of others was now a death sentence. Democracy was still in full swing, but criminals didn't get a free walk as they once did. There were not enough people to maintain lawbreakers in prisons anymore so a swifter justice had to be handed down.

The police were now able to make the hard decisions, saving the time and energy of lengthy trials. But as before, they would only take matters into their hands when it was a clear cut case, such as the one now happening at the bank.

Which was where the zombies came in.

The SWAT team moved back behind the ghouls once the shooting had stopped and with a cattle prod to the back of the first ghoul, the others were lead up the stairs single file. The rope held them as one group swaying back and forth between them and sometimes going taut when one moved too far in front of the one behind it. They were a mottled bunch, a few missing limbs or eyes. One had no face, only a jagged hole where its sinus glistened in the sun. This one was last in line and only managed to get where it needed to by being pulled along like a pet. For what the ghouls were being used for they didn't need to be pretty.

At the glass doors to the bank, one of the SWAT officers set a small plastic timer on the doorframe, right over where the locks were. Then he stepped back and pressed a small switch on a black box in his hand. There was a soft poof and a puff of smoke appeared where the lock had been and then the SWAT officer opened the doors, the locking mechanism blown away without so much as breaking the safety glass of the doors. The man knew his trade.

One at a time the zombies were herded into the bank, and they were now followed by all the SWAT officers, each one decked out in black with Kevlar and black boots. All carried M-16's, and a few had Browning pump action shotguns.

Half the police squad of regular cops also went up the stairs to cover both sides of the doors. They wouldn't enter until told to do so.

As the zombies entered the bank, the first ghoul in line wore something extra on its ball cap. It was a tiny camera, and as the ghoul moved through the lobby, moving its head back and forth slowly like it was an automatic scanner, the lens on its cap was recording the room.

Just inside the glass doors, the SWAT team waited while one officer held a small monitor in his hands, studying the layout of the bank.

And just like the officers knew would happen, the bank robbers tipped their hand, coming out from behind the teller windows and two more jumping out from behind desks set off to the side for loan applications.

They carried mean looking assault rifles, and like it had been choreographed in advance, they began spraying the zombies, bullets slicing into the rotting flesh to leave jagged, oozing lines of pus and ichor.

The zombies were cannon fodder, sent in to soak up as much of the ammunition as the foolish bank robbers wanted to expend.

The four hardened criminals were so busy shooting the ghouls they never noticed when more zombies entered the bank by the rear fire exit.

There had been a police car in the back alley with two men guarding the exit in case the bank robbers tried to escape, but both men were now lying on the ground, very dead. Their insides had been ripped out and their necks and faces had been shredded by teeth. Blood pooled under their bodies and flies had already begun feeding on the congealing plasma.

To the left of the corpses was the open fire door, the door swaying back and forth on its hinges. The last form had just entered, a few drops of blood still dripping from the body part the figure held as it chewed happily.

Inside the bank, the robbers turned to see more zombies entering, but their eyes went wide when they saw there was something very different about these ghouls.

For starters, four of them were armed with firearms taken from the dead cops in the alley. Jonah was in the lead, and as the bank robbers turned to defend themselves, Jonah and his three undead brothers began shooting at them.

Bullets ripped into the criminal's chests, shattering rib cages and shredding hearts. In less than thirty seconds the battle was over for the simple reason the bank robbers had to duck down to avoid being shot while Jonah and his brothers swarmed forward, heedless of the bullet impacts on their bodies.

Jonah felt a slug tug the sleeve of his left arm, but he was driven by the desire to be free, so he pushed forward, shooting one man in the face three times, pulverizing his features as the robber flopped to the ground.

As soon as the body hit the floor, another ghoul was leaning over him. First the ghoul leaned down and began feeding, but no sooner did it begin this, then Jonah grabbed the ghoul by the scruff of its collar and dragged it off the dead man. He pointed to the fallen automatic and the ghoul nodded, understanding.

There would be time for feeding later; right now they needed to wipe out any humans in the building.

When the four bank robbers were down and bleeding out on the polished stone floor, Jonah gathered his small force. There were fifteen other ghouls besides him, but he now had a dozen more to add to his army. Though they had dozens of bullet holes, the bank robbers had been foolish, not shooting the ghouls in the head, assuming they only had to shoot the torsos such as on a human body.

Jonah turned to a ghoul, then made some quick hand signs. Hanging from his belt was the cattle prod, and when the ghoul he had gestured to returned a minute later with a pitcher of water, Jonah quickly doused the first ghoul in line, the one with the camera on its head.

The camera and ball cap were tossed to the ground, but it still continued recording, the SWAT officers watching fascinated. Jonah wetted their heads and then used the cattle prod, awakening the dead brain to each zombie and adding one more fighter to his campaign.

He did this eleven more times, and when he was through, he turned to his undead brothers and sisters and pointed to the main doors of the bank.

With more than half now armed with powerful firearms, Jonah led them to the glass doors.

He was the first to see the SWAT officer peering inside the bank with his mouth hanging open.

Before the cop could do more than yelp in surprise, Jonah shot him through the glass, the safety glass shattering and the SWAT officer falling away to roll down the steps. Blood pumped from his sucking chest wound and he gasped, a bubbly froth seeping from the corner of his mouth.

The other SWAT officers saw their fallen man and turned with weapons blazing, firing at the oncoming ghouls.

What had been a simple bank robbery was turning into something else and no man on the police force was prepared for it.

Bullets blew through bodies like they were made of paper and only the ghouls with head shots went down for good. But for those three destroyed zombies, all the SWAT were gunned down, even their Kevlar vests no match for the onslaught of slugs that seemed to find every crevice and chink in their arms and necks.

Jonah stood on the landing of the bank, the stairs leading down to the street, and he gazed at the other police officers while they were staring back at him dumfounded.

Jonah managed to crack a smile then, but on his dead rotting face it was a rictus of death.

He raised his gun and tried to yell, but all that came out was a moan.

The other ghouls behind him took up the moan and a high-pitched wailing filled the air, chilling every living human on the street.

Then Jonah charged down the stairs, firing at the shocked cops. But these were men who had been trained to fight when attacked and they soon shook off their stupor and began firing back, a half dozen of Jonah's ghouls being gunned down in a fraction of a minute. But there were too many to shoot, and as the zombies shuffled down the stairs like old men, it was an odd sight. Automatic rifle fire pierced the air to rend living flesh from bone. One cop received a bullet to the eye, the orb popping like an over-cooked hardboiled egg.

The round pulped his brain to mush and took out a large chunk of scalp, the man in blue dropping to the street.

Jonah's people moved onto the street, now mixing in between the cars.

A squad car went up in a blazing fireball from a stray round, five ghouls getting caught in the blast. Their dry bodies began to burn like kindling and they moved about the street, flailing their limbs widely, the immolated bodies now nothing but walking crematoriums.

The blazing torches of human flesh tried to walk a few more feet, but soon dropped to the earth, the charred skulls and gaping mouths smoldering to ash.

Jonah screamed in rage, the sound coming out like another wail. He was losing men, but he knew there were plenty more to find when he was finished here.

One cop shot a ghoul, but the bullet went right through the frail form, continuing out the back to hit another cop. That man dropped to the street, dead, never knowing it was friendly fire that was sending him to Hell.

In less than a minute the battle was over, the ghouls now swarming over the remaining men and women while they tried to fight off the undead attackers.

The cops guns were taken from their dead hands to then be used on the other policemen, and the ghouls were then allowed to feed on the corpses now that the fight was over. The sickening sounds of ripping flesh, cracking bones and rib cages being torn open like a hungry man eating a lobster filled the street while Jonah stood over it all, surveying the carnage he had wrought.

He heard the distinct sound of whimpering from his right side and a little behind him. Moving to the police car, he looked over the sill of the open door to see a police woman cowering there. Her gun had cycled dry and it was clear she was petrified. A wet spot was on her pants between her thighs and she was huddling in a small, yellow pool of water.

"Please don't kill me, please, I have a family," she squeaked as tears rolled down her cheeks.

Jonah opened his mouth, wanting to tell her that so did he at one time, but now they were nothing but dust, but of course nothing came out but a few guttural grunts.

Deciding there was really no point to it anyway, he raised the gun in his hand and shot the woman in the head. Blowing out the right side of her face and splattering her brains across the road.

Her body dropped to the pavement and began to twitch like it was electrified and Jonah grunted to another two ghouls, who came like good soldiers should. He pointed to the dead woman, her fingers still twitching slightly, and gestured they could feed.

The two ghouls nodded and went to their knees, tearing into the woman like she was a banquet.

Jonah watched for a few seconds, and when one of the ghouls turned and handed him the woman's heart, Jonah took it, tearing into the strong muscle with his brown teeth, blood dripping down his chin to fall onto his coveralls.

He was a warrior now, feeding on the heart of his vanquished enemy, and when he was finished with this city, he would feast on the heart of every human he could find.

With the sounds of the undead mob feasting, slurping gurgling noises filling the air, Jonah looked up and grinned.

This was a good start to his campaign, and when he was finished, the blood of the humans would run red in the streets and he and his brothers and sisters would be free at last, even if he had to slaughter every living being on the planet to do so.

Chapter 6

The movie was just getting out and Marsha, Chad and Robert stepped out into the sunlight, blinking as their eyes adjusted to the light.

Around them, people passed them by as they talked about the movies and what they liked or disliked about the films. A few zombies moved about, one washing the windows of a nearby building while another was handing out restaurant coupons.

"Man, those movies are great," Chad said as he began shadow boxing as the trio walked down the street. "I could do that if I wanted to."

"Sure you could," Robert said with a grin. "I bet you could be the champ, too."

"Hell, yes, I could," Chad agreed and then when he saw the look of sarcasm on Robert's face, he scowled.

"Oh, shit, you're just messin' with me, huh."

"No," Robert said, his tone dripping with yet more sarcasm, "I think you could be the heavy weight champion of the world."

"I can kick your ass, at least," Chad said and then he turned and darted in next to Robert, his left fist swinging out playfully. He connected with Robert's side, but he pulled the punch, but he did make a loud *oomph* sound, like he'd connected with a haymaker.

"Oh, he's down now!" Chad called. "He's gonna put him down for good!"

"Will you two grow up for five minutes, please?" Marsha said while she walked behind the two men.

"Aww, we're just havin' fun, Marsha, why don't you join in," Chad said and he pretended like he was going to hit her. She crossed her arms in front of her and glared at him in a, *I dare you* look. Chad lowered his arm and mumbled sorry.

Marsha turned to Robert who was a few feet ahead of her.

"I need to get home for dinner soon, Robert, are you going to take me or what?"

"Sure, I can do that," Robert told her, "then me and Chad are gonna go see that red-head he's been seein', right, Chad?"

"You know it, buddy," Chad said while smiling widely, thinking of the girl he'd been tapping for the past two weeks.

Marsha frowned a little, but then she wiped it off her lips. She didn't want Chad to see her reacting to what Robert had said. She didn't know why she liked the big ape so much, but she did.

They rounded the movie theater and headed for Robert's car, the red paint reflecting the light like a mirror. Robert admired the paint job, flicked a small piece of dust off the door, and jumped in, the others following.

A few cars were also pulling out of the parking lot, but in less than a minute Robert was driving down the street, his arm hanging off the sill of the door once more.

Chad leaned forward and turned the dial to the radio, wanting to hear some music, but all he got was the news.

After some static, a voice, deep with seriousness, began speaking.

"...And it's unknown at this time exactly what has happened, but reports of what appears to be an uprising of the dead, as ridiculous as that sounds, is in effect. What began as a bank robbery has turned into a massacre and even now the authorities are trying to weed through the wreckage in an attempt to figure out what has occurred. Reports of a large group of zombies leaving the scene of the incident has been reported, but thus far, anyone who was near the actual sight of the attacks is either dead by gunshot or has been torn apart with what appears to be teeth and claws. We'll keep you informed of the situation, but for now all citizens are warned to stay away from Broadway…" Chad turned the tuner on the radio, bored with the chatter, music now coming from the speakers.

"Hey, I wanted to hear that," Robert said annoyed.

"Why? It's just something about a bank robbery. Doesn't affect us, does it?"

"No," Robert replied, "I guess not, but it sounded interesting. Nothing ever exciting happens in the city anymore, ya know."

"Yeah, well, I can live with that just fine, buddy. The last time something interesting happened was five years ago and everyone died. No, man, nice and peaceful is just fine with me."

Robert didn't answer, his mind now on things of the past. Marsha felt the same thing. Chad bringing up the plague always did that to her. Memories of Seth, her parents and friends would haunt her till the day she died. Sure, she had moved on, but only as a coping mechanism. Many times she would still cry herself to sleep, though she would never tell the two idiots sitting in front of her.

Robert slowed at a red light and waited for it to change. Across the street were two zombies. They had trash bags and small grabbers and they were moving down the street, picking up trash. Robert shook his head as he watched the pitiful creatures. He didn't know why he hated them with such passion but he did. It was just something he couldn't explain. Every time he saw one of them it reminded him of everything he had lost.

He had heard stories of people who had gone to a store, or to eat, and had looked up to see a zombie who had been a relative. He always wondered how that must feel. To be eating a steak at a nice restaurant and to glance up and realize the bus boy had once been your father, or brother.

Of course it made sense. The zombies had been human once and had families who loved them. The ghouls were husbands, wives, brothers and sisters. They had mothers and fathers and children. He had been told all ghouls from a particular city were placed in other cities to lessen the chance a loved one would see a zombie that was known to them, but in any bureaucracy mistakes are made and it was always possible to run into a dead relative.

That made Robert cringe, and when the light changed he drove on, looking away from the two ghouls as he sped down the street. He was about a mile from the Broadway bank and he realized the car in front of him was slowing down. Deciding he didn't feel like waiting, he sped up, passing the car and swerving back into the lane. The woman in the other car honked at him waving her fist in the air, but he ignored it, Chad whooping it up in fun.

Robert took the next intersection hard and he let out a yelp of surprise to see it was full of people, a large crowd moving down the street.

No wait, he realized, they weren't people, they were deadheads! And they had to be more than fifty of them, all moving down the street like a mob.

That was when the first gunshot rang out and the windshield on the car shattered. Not knowing what to do, he slammed on the brakes, the car idling in the middle of the road

"Holy shit, what the hell's going on?" Chad yelled as he ducked down.

Marsha ducked, too, but she still didn't know what was happening.

"I don't know, but there's a shitload of deadheads in the street," Robert gasped.

Then Robert saw a woman running down the street to the right of the mob. He couldn't believe his eyes when he saw the deadheads shoot her, riddling her body with bullets.

That didn't make sense. Deadheads didn't know how to use guns.

No sooner did the woman go down then a half-dozen ghouls swarmed over her still warm corpse, ripping her to pieces in seconds.

Realizing he needed to leave now, Robert swung the car around and drove off, his foot planted firmly on the gas pedal.

Then another gunshot sounded, followed by the staccato of an automatic weapon. The pavement was chewed up as the bullets walked up until the rounds reached the car, the left rear tire deflating as five rounds found it.

Robert lost control and the car swerved to the left, heading directly for a zombie that was walking a dog.

The dog, realizing it was in danger, ripped free from the ghoul, dashing off down the street while its leash trailed behind it. But the ghoul wasn't as fast or as quick, and before it could move, the car was smashing into it, knocking the body to the street and running over it. The corpse was ripped apart as the undercarriage pulled and tore at the rotted flesh, and when the car had passed, there was nothing but a bloody lump of meat lying in the road.

Robert tried to straighten the vehicle, but before he could compensate, he crashed into a lamp post, the front end of his car wrapping around the pole like a lover's arms. The metal pole bent to the right and the bulb shattered, raining small crystals down on the heads of the three passengers.

The air bags went off and Robert and Chad were pummeled by the force of the air bags erupting from their cocoons, but Marsha had no such protection. Her body was thrown forward to bounce off the back of the front seat like a rag doll, her neck almost snapping forward with enough force to break it. But it wasn't enough and she bounced off the soft padding to fall to the floor, her mind now dazed and confused.

While the occupants of the now wrecked car lay dazed, falling in and out of consciousness, the zombie mob slowly grew closer, with only murder on their dead minds.

Chapter 7

Marsha barely felt herself being removed from the car, strong hands pulling her free. Her head lolled to the side lazily, and if it wasn't for the bruise on her forehead, she would have looked like she was sleeping.

From down the street, another gunshot rang out, striking the side panel of the car. Steam drifted up from under the bent hood, the radiator now cracked and draining green fluid onto the street like a hemorrhaging artery.

Marsha moaned, not understanding what was happening, and as she struggled to wake up, she could hear more gunshots from in front of her. No wait, they were really from behind, or were they?

She was all mixed up, but when she opened her eyes, she realized she was being dragged by someone, and she could see what was behind her as the heels of her sneakers slowly bounced on the sidewalk.

"Stay still, you've been in a car crash, I've got you," a man's voice said from behind her, or really in front of her. Her stomach felt like it wanted to expel the lunch of burgers and fries and the world spun like she was on a merry-go-round.

Her vision cleared for a moment and she could see Robert's car ten feet away and still moving as she was dragged away. She reached out a hand to Chad and Robert, but it was barely lifted, her strength not returned yet.

She could hear more gunshots, but they sounded muffled, and then, though her vision was blurry, she saw a bullet strike Robert in the back of the head as he lay slumped over the steering wheel. There was a popping sound and a large spray of blood erupted from Robert's scalp to splatter onto the inside of the windshield. The body jerked for a moment and Marsha saw something spinning in the air. It was only later when she replayed the incident in her head that she realized it had been a large piece of Robert's skull.

More gunshots filled the air and Chad's body, slumped to the side, his eyes wide open in death, began to jump and dance as round after round pummeled his corpse. If the man had survived the crash, he would certainly be dead now.

It was just as Marsha was being dragged around the corner of a building and into an alley, that she glimpsed the first of the ghouls descend on her two friends corpses. In the blink of an eye she saw the zombies tear into the bodies, teeth biting deep and ripping arms from sockets with bloody tendrils of muscle dripping like baby drool.

If she had been more conscious of what was actually happening she had no doubt she would have been screaming to them, despite her friends already being dead, but in her altered state of semi-consciousness, all she could do was record the images and then replay them over and over in her head.

The last thing she saw before she was dragged around into the alleyway was the severed head of Chad being held aloft by a ghoul wearing an orange vest. Chad's mouth was hanging open, the tongue now gone, one of the ghouls already ripping into it to feed on the soft tissue within. Chad's eyes were still open, the white and blue orbs reflecting the sun like tiny mirrors, and then the head was lost in the reaching hands of the undead crowd as they dug deep into the open neck to pull out the brains within.

Mercifully, as Marsha was dragged into the shadows of the alley, she lost consciousness again, only now, with the images of her slaughtered friends to haunt her, she was plagued with visions of death and horror.

*   *   *

Jonah stared at his new army and shook his head slowly.

While at first the undead had seemed to be more intelligent after he had shocked them, it was painfully obvious that whatever had somehow given him back his thoughts was not going to work on others of his kind.

While it seemed the initial shock did seem to bring clarity to the ghouls, as time passed they slipped back into that fugue state between life and death.

There was one thing that did seem to work to his advantage. Though their intelligence slid back to that of a two-year-old, they still seemed to remember that he was their leader.

So while they couldn't shoot weapons or think in any constructive way, they could follow simple orders by using sign language.

It was terribly obvious if he was not in charge they would end up turning into a raging mob of feeding zombies with only one thing on their dead minds.

To feed on any human being they could find.

But though Jonah had no problem with that, the takeover of the city was something to be done in stages. If he simply let loose his undead army on the unsuspecting populace, they would be gunned down and destroyed in no time.

So for now he would have to slow down and watch how things played out. It seemed for more than a half a day after being shocked a ghoul would be receptive to using a gun or other weapon and thinking for itself, but then it would slide back into stupidity.

So he would have to gauge when and where he shocked his new recruits, not wanting to waste his resources. He had already tried to re-shock the stupid ones but all he ended up doing was melting their brains.

No, whatever had happened to him was an anomaly and he would just have to accept that he was alone in his revolution. Though his undead brethren didn't understand, he knew he was doing what was best for them. They would be slaves no longer, and if it was the last thing he did in this life, or death, so to speak, he would see that one thing came to pass.

*   *   *

Marsha came awake with a start.

Her head was killing her and for a moment she didn't know where she was. But then images of Robert and Chad being killed flooded her mind and she gasped, not believing it had actually happened.

She looked around and saw she was in an alley. From somewhere nearby she could hear the sounds of gunshots and screams. She was lying on the ground, and when she tried to move, her left hand pressed into something goopy and warm.

Her heart leapt to her throat and she had visions of dead bodies, her hand now wrist deep in rotten organs and offal, but when she turned her head, she saw it was nothing more than dog poop. Though not the most aromatic odor in the world, at least it was mundane and harmless. Slowly, she scraped her palm on the ground until she had most of it off, and then she wiped the rest on her shirt, at the moment not caring about her clothing being clean. Her dress was hiked up a little and she grabbed the hem and brought it back down. Her legs were dirty and a few scrapes could be seen here and there on her creamy white skin, but she looked and felt intact.

She sat up, wondering what she was going to do, not com-prehending how she had ended up in an alley. The last real thought she had was of being in the car before it crashed, humanoid shapes appearing at the end of the alley. With the sun at their backs, she couldn't see who they were, but their slow, ungainly movements gave her an idea to their identity.

She tried to get to her feet, but her legs gave out and her head began to swim, threatening her with a fainting spell. Her vision swam and she knew deep down inside if she passed out she was dead.

Knowing she had to move, she began crawling away from the shambling bodies behind her. She kept waiting to hear a gunshot and feel a sharp pain in her back, but nothing came.

On hands and knees she moved, hoping to reach the opposite end of the alley. And then what?

Why did she think the other end would be her salvation?

But she tried, her instinct to survive carrying her on, but though she did her best, the ghouls behind her slowly grew closer until the first one was almost leaning over her.

She rolled over then, some small part of her wanting to see it coming, and she gazed up and into the undead eyes of a zombie. This one wore a housecoat and had once been a butler, but now it was just another ghoul. Its face was covered in congealing blood and the front of its chest was awash with red as if the ghoul had drank tomato juice and had ended up spilling the entire can on itself instead of drinking it.

With a low, guttural moan, it reached down with its pale, cracked hands to grab her, while behind it four more followed suit.

Not knowing what to do, she let out a squeak, the fear in her chest too strong to let her scream, and she prepared herself to die.

But as she closed her eyes and waited, she heard a meaty *thunk* and then felt cold raindrops splatter her face. Opening her eyes, she looked up to see the ghoul had stopped his attempt to grab her, and the reason was the large lead pipe now sticking out of the top of its head. The other end of the pipe was being held by a man in a policeman's uniform, and as she watched in stunned fascination, the cop yanked the pipe out of the pulped head and swung it back for another strike. As he did this, bits of brain matter flew off the tip of the pipe to splatter onto the ground. Then he was charging at the next ghoul in line, swinging the pipe like a bat, the side of the zombie's head caving in like a hollowed-out eggshell.

The right eye of the ghoul popped out of its socket from the blow and it flew through the air like a golf ball to land near Marsha. As she looked down at the small orb, she could have sworn the pupil swiveled to look at her, but then the policeman had taken a step back and the heel of his shoes came down on the eye, flattening it to white paste.

Marsha could only watch in horror as the cop swung the pipe for all he was worth, pulping faces and cracking skulls. When he was through, his breath coming in gasps, more than half a dozen bodies littered the alleyway.

But there were more approaching and these ghouls carried guns. As a few stray rounds struck the alley wall, the man reached over and grabbed Marsha by the left arm, dragging her up and off the ground.

Bullets pockmarked the brick walls to the sides, but all missed, though one round went so close to the cop's face he felt the air move in its passing.

Then they were back in the sun, now on the next street, and he was dragging her like he was a parent and she an errant child acting up at the shopping mall.

Marsha let him pull her for more than fifty feet, but by now she had gotten a little bit of her balance back and she was becoming upset by everything that had happened. She thought back to Chad and Robert, remembering how they had been attacked, but that was before she had passed out. Maybe she had imagined the entire thing. After all, how could Chad and Robert be dead? And by the zombies? The same gentile slaves that did everything from cut her grass to wash her car? No, it didn't make sense.

As the two moved down the street, Marsha suddenly stopped running as they passed a clothing store, and the cop was almost yanked off his feet when she became a lead weight as he pulled her along behind him.

"What the hell are you stopping for? We have to keep moving," he snapped at her, his face red from exertion.

"Why? Why do we have to keep moving? What the hell is going on around here? Why did those deadheads attack my friends, we need to go back there and help them and how could they be using guns. And who the fuck are you?"

"I'm Brian, Brian Purcell, and I'm a cop if you haven't figured that out yet," he said breathlessly, his eyes looking past her shoulder at the opening to the alley. It was wreathed in shadows, the tall walls on either side keeping the sunlight from penetrating the darkness. It was as he watched the opening he saw the first of the ghouls emerging. They were pale and rotting like all of their kind, only these zombies carried guns. Brian still hadn't fully accepted that, but he had seen it already plain as day and knew if he didn't accept it, that very fact could mean his death.

"I know you're a goddamn cop, buddy. But I want to know what the fuck is happening and I'm not gonna move until you tell me what's going on." She crossed her arms in front of her like a spoiled child and Brian stared at her as if she was crazy.

No, she wasn't crazy; she was just like hundreds of the remaining citizens in the city that refused to believe what was happening.

As hard to fathom as it was, it appeared the zombies were revolting. Somehow, they had learned to fire weapons and most seemed to have a modicum of intelligence. But he had been at the massacre at the bank and had been lucky enough to escape with his life, slinking away with his tail between his legs. But he was no fool, and when all his brothers in blue had been killed and then eaten, he had hightailed it away from the carnage, not looking back until he was two blocks away. His 9mm Glock was empty; he'd expended every round trying to stop the rampaging ghouls but it had done no good. It was only when he had fired one of his last rounds that he saw a head come apart and the ghoul went down for good.

That was when he realized headshots appeared to be the only way to take the deadheads down and keep them down. But after using up his remaining bullets, he had no choice but to run for it. His act of cowardice still ate at his gut like a belly full of rats but he knew if he had tried to be brave like in some old movie, he would have only ended up as dead as the rest of the men on the defending police force.

With a sigh, he quickly filled Marsha in with short, clipped sentences, about what had happened to him and what he thought was happening to the city, and when he finished, she stared at him as if he had grown a third eye.

"What? That's crazy," she said. "Deadheads are stupid. They can barely do the functions they're trained to do; they can't do a fraction of what you're suggesting."

"Oh, really?" Brian said. "Then how do you explain that?" He pointed over her shoulder and Marsha turned to see more than a score of ghouls emerging from the alleyway. She was about to open her mouth, try to explain what she was seeing with her very own eyes when a shot rang out and the store window to her left shattered, spraying small bits of cube-sized glass onto her and Brian.

"Shit, they're shooting at us, come on, damn it. If you don't want to come then I'm leaving you, 'cause I'm not gonna die for some idiot who doesn't want to accept what's right in front of her face!"

"Hey, I'm not an idiot!" She snapped back while stomping her foot, but this time when Brian grabbed her right hand and began running, she didn't fight him, the two dashing down the street while a hail of bullets followed them. Brian felt something sting his side, like a giant wasp had burrowed under his shirt, but he ignored it, concentrating on running. As they moved through the streets, leaving the mob of zombies behind, more ghouls could be seen on the sidewalks, and it was only when Brian slowed and watched them that he realized they weren't like the others shooting at him. These deadheads were like the ones from the day before, simple automatons doing a specified job.

Brian held up his hand for Marsha to be careful, and the two moved to the middle of the street, wanting to stay clear of the ghouls despite his confidence they were harmless.

The two crept by the zombies, Brian never removing his gaze, and in seconds they were past and moving on. All around them other civilians were running here and there, some with backpacks and boxes of food and items of personal attachment. It seemed in less than half a day the city was already falling into chaos. With the cops either slaughtered or abandoning their posts to be with their families, there was no one to maintain control and the city was falling into a state of lawlessness which it hadn't seen since Bloody V had arrived and wiped out so many.

"So if the deadheads are crazy now then why didn't those attack us?" Marsha asked, referring to the ghouls they had just passed.

"How the hell should I know?" Brian replied. "All I know is that some of them are on the attack and if they catch you, you're dead; then eaten like food."

"So then I didn't imagine what happened to Robert and..."

"No, you didn't," he replied. "It happened, and if I hadn't gotten to you when I did, you'd be dead now, too."

Marsha swallowed the knot in her throat as they walked down the center of the street. All around them people were running, a few driving past them with vehicles piled high with suitcases. But it was already apparent the roads leading out of the city would be choked with cars or blocked. All it would take was one vehicle to break down or stall and the entire infrastructure would crumble, like when drivers slowed down to see a particularly nasty accident on the highway. The traffic would extend for miles just because a few gawkers wanted to glimpse some blood that wasn't theirs.

Brian turned a corner and Marsha slowed as they approached a police car parked in the street, its front tires on the sidewalk. The doors were open and the red and blue lights on top spun impotently, the bright light of the day helping to diffuse their impact on the scene. As the couple moved closer, Marsha could see the doors and inside of the squad car was bathed in blood. It was everywhere, still dripping from the headliner and windshield like someone had tossed a gallon of bright scarlet paint on and into the car as a prank. But as she got closer still, the coppery odor of blood came to her nose and she realized some bad shit had gone down here. There had to be at least seven to eight pints of blood splattered around the car, and if a human being, even two of them, had lost that much, there was no way they could still be alive.

"Careful, we don't know what's on the other side of the cruiser," Brian said as he leaned in to inspect the inside. His eyes darted to the radio on the dash, but when he saw the mike had been ripped out of the jack, wires now exposed, he knew there would be no way he could use it. The next thing he searched for were guns, or better yet, bullets for his empty Glock, but there was nothing. The cruiser had been stripped of everything worth taking and it was only when he saw something lying on the passenger floorboard that he realized for sure what had happened here.

Reaching over the blood-soaked seat, he picked up the object he had found. Marsha stood behind him, her eyes darting back and forth every time someone ran past them. She kept expecting one of the passersby to reach out and attack her, like in one of those apocalyptic movies where everyone became crazy.

Brian's back was to her as he leaned into the car, and when he backed out, she saw he was holding something.

"You find something?" Marsha asked.

"Yeah, sort of," he whispered.

Slowly, he turned around and showed her what he'd found.

"Is that...? No, it can't be."

He nodded that it was.

Marsha's pupils went wide and she let out a soft squeak as she stared at the bloody thing in his hand, as if it couldn't be true, that it had to be a joke, like fake vomit or plastic dog poop.

But as she looked at the human heart in Brian's hand, the blood coating the muscle glistening in the sun, and the coppery aroma of blood now becoming stronger, she knew it was the truth.

Though she would have done anything to stop herself, she felt her vision swimming, and before she realized it, she was passing out, the horrors of the past fifteen minutes simply too much for her fragile mind to take.

"Hey, are you...?" She heard Brian ask from far away. Then she was swallowed by darkness, and as she slipped into the oblivion waiting for her, she had to admit she welcomed it.

Chapter 8

Jonah glanced over his shoulder to see over two hundred zombies following him down the center of the street, more than half with guns or clubs. Every ghoul was covered in blood as they had been feeding on what remained of the population of the city while they moved through the streets.

Moving around an intersection, Jonah slowed and raised his left hand into the air to stop his followers.

In front of him, blocking the street, were three police cars and two military jeeps, the beginning of more military troops that would come later, no doubt.

Behind the blockade were three news vans, the men and women now aiming their cameras at Jonah and his brothers and sisters.

Behind him, his undead brethren swayed back and forth, a few still snacking on bloody body parts of what were once human beings.

His recruitment had gone better than he had hoped and in less than half a day he had collected and transformed two hundred dead men and women, and he had no doubt by the next day he would have three times that. As they moved through the city, he had teams now shocking the new recruits. Though many had reverted back to stupid animals, there were always fresh ghouls who retained enough intelligence to do what he needed them to do. By the time they had become merely stupid zombies again, there was more to replace them.

But even as undead idiots, they knew how to fight. Feeding on the living had become a compunction by every ghoul who tasted the sweet flesh of the living. Once imbibing of the living tissue, every zombie felt revitalized and strong. And the meat seemed to add to their strength as most ghouls were twice as strong as before, which would bring them on par with an average human male.

Rotting tissue was still a concern, but even this seemed to have slowed slightly, the fresh blood seeming to be an undead version of the fountain of youth.

The sounds of gunshots filled the street almost immediately and ghouls became pockmarked with bullets. Jonah pointed to the blockade, and with a guttural growl, aimed his army to attack. Though he moved to the side to get out of the way, his undead horde surged forward, only carnage and blood on their dull minds. Jonah would not be in the phalanx of the attack for fear of being shot. Because he was more intelligent, he had a distinct knowledge of not wanting to sustain bodily harm. He knew if he received too much damage then he could possibly die...again. And he most definitely didn't want that to happen.

So he let his army surge forward, the first wave soaking up bullets like it was horizontal rain.

Thirty ghouls were shot to pieces in seconds, but while they went down, it gave the others more time to move out to the sides of the street and then charge forward. The police and the soldiers fought valiantly, but in the end it was never a question of who would win. When you're battling an army that feels no pain, never tires or has compassion, they will always overcome in the end.

As the police ran out of bullets and tried to reload, and while the other men and women tried to cover them, the army of ghouls swarmed over them until there were so many bodies huddled in the area together, attacker and defender alike, to shoot at them would be suicide to the other policemen.

Which what had happened on more than one occasion. A young rookie, the woman barely out of the academy by a year, swiveled to her left and shot an old woman with a missing left eye and half her face rotted away. But the thin body couldn't stop the heavy round and the bullet went through the thin frame and then continued on into the policeman on the other side of her.

The cop jerked forward, not understanding what had happened to him, but no sooner was he shot, then five zombies attacked him, forcing him to the pavement with his shrieks of agony filling the air. The policeman was grabbed by his arms and legs, another ghoul grabbing his head, and as one team they all pulled, twisting like they were wishing on a wishbone. The man was drawn and quartered; his limbs tearing off, the tissue stretching like bloody elastics as he screamed for someone to end his pain.

But he wasn't dead yet. With all his limbs off he was still alive, his blood shooting out of the jagged wounds in quarts. It was only when the ghoul who had hold of his head began to twist, and twist some more that his neck snapped and he died. But the ghoul wanted the head and so twisted again and again until the now weakened spine had cracked and the skin had turned into a knot. The head popped off, a small amount of blood leaking out of the wound, and the zombie moved away with its prize. As for the torso, it was torn apart, the warm organs pulled from the open tears to be devoured by the hungry mob. A few gnawed on the ribcage like they were at a barbecue, the blood lathering their chin and chest like the thickest, reddest barbecue sauce in history. When the ghouls were finished there was only a few tatters of bloody rags of flesh to remain, plus a few bones with teeth marks to prove the man had existed at all.

As for the policewoman who shot him, she almost suffered a similar fate. As she shot at the attacking zombies, it was only a matter of time before she ran out of bullets. Dropping the gun with no time to reload, she pulled a long knife from her hip. It wasn't regulation, but her father had given it to her and she had told him she would carry it. As the ghoul came for her, she stabbed her attacker in the chest, the long blade sliding deep into the zombie's heart. She expected the ghoul to die then, to fall to the pavement as it expelled its last breath of air. But as the zombie ignored the blade and reached for her, she realized she wasn't dealing with a living foe and so would have to change her tactics.

Knocking its pale hands away from her, she grabbed the hilt of the blade and pulled it free of the chest, the sucking sound causing her to wince. Then with a spin, she used all her momentum to slash the blade across the ghoul's neck. The razor's edge split the dried flesh like it was paper and a black ichor seeped out to drench the front of the dead man, but still it continued its attack.

"Oh, shit, Christie, you're in big trouble," she mumbled to herself.

But the ghoul didn't stop coming for her and she backed a step away, her boot squishing into the body cavity of one of her fellow officers. She glanced down and saw it was Tony Carvello. The man had been a wiseass, always having a joke to say about everything. He had always had a grin on his face that said he knew something you didn't and had tried to get Christie to go on a date with him for weeks, but she had always shot him down. She glanced at his corpse and saw Tony's mouth was wide open and the tongue was missing, torn off and devoured by some hungry ghoul. Though her stomach heaved and she felt sorrow for the dead man, she knew she had to focus on herself or she would be joining him soon. Tony's gun was near his corpse, only a few inches from his outstretched hand, the first three fingers missing, teeth marks showing where they had been chewed off, and she reached down and grabbed it, then had to fall back as the ghoul with the slashed neck came for her. She stumbled and fell over Tony's legs and her back hit the pavement hard and she closed her mouth, not wanting to bite off her tongue. That would be a laugh, to be battling the dead only to bite her own tongue off by accident and bleed to death while the battle swirled around her.

The sounds of guns, screams and other sounds of war filled her senses as she stared at the legs and bodies now above her. It was horrendous; it was something she would never have believed possible. As she lay on her back, she realized this wasn't a defense of the city, this was a complete massacre and the humans were losing.

Then her reverie was cut short when the ghoul with the neck wound fell on top of her, its teeth clacking together like fake dentist's teeth chattering again and again.

She reached up with her free hand and forced the snapping jaws away from her, her hand sinking into the soft flesh which resembled putty more than skin. Her other hand now held Tony's .38, and she jammed the muzzle into the belly of the ghoul, firing it three times. The first shot was muffled, but the second two blasts filled the area around her as the bullets tore through flesh and bone and blasted a hole out the back of the ghoul. But the zombie never noticed the wounds, and though she was doing her best to stop it, she knew she had very little time left. Then another ghoul spotted her and moved forward, wanting to join in on the action. It fell down by her feet and tried to bite her thigh, but she kicked it in the nose and it rolled away, but soon came crawling back. She knew this was it. Christie Kendall was about to die.

Then another policeman was by her side and he reached down and pulled the zombie off her, then kicked the other at her feet in the face, smashing cartilage and pulverizing bone. The ghoul rolled away and Christie looked up to see her sergeant gazing down on her, but no sooner did she open her mouth to tell him thank you, then three more ghouls charged at him, knocking him over as he screamed for help. Christie dropped back to the pavement, the gun skittering from her hand. The sergeant's carotid artery was ripped out by brown teeth, and as blood geysered into the air like a fountain, Christie realized her savior had become a victim.

Scrabbling away on her hands and knees, she moved to one of the SWAT vans and crawled underneath it. As she hid under the vehicle, she whimpered in fear and watched the destruction of the people who had been her friends and co-workers. A young cop with bright red hair was tackled by three dead women and a zombie dressed like a delivery boy. As he went down, his shrieks filled the air and Christie had to turn away from the visceral sight as four sets of teeth sank into the screaming man's face, tearing off his skin like it was taffy. Another cop, an old veteran, was brought down by his own clumsiness and weight. The man was fat, and as he tripped over the corpse of a ghoul, he fell heavily to the road, his face smashing so hard he broke his own nose in a bloody froth of scarlet. He tried to roll over like a turtle on its back, and when he did, he stared up at the growling, pale faces of five zombies.

Like wild animals they pounced on the fat cop, teeth and nails digging in like they were dogs digging for bones. The man screamed long and loud, but soon his screams were gargled with blood as he spit a vermilion froth across the road and into the faces of the closet ghouls. They never noticed, but began ripping the fat cop's insides out while the man shrieked and slowly died. It was only when his heart was pulled from his chest that he finally expired, but like he was a carcass in the wild, the zombies gathered around him like coyotes, feeding on the red chunks of his flesh, bits and gobbets of meat slipping from their hands and mouths to fall back onto the dead cop's face.

Christie was crying now, her body shaking with fear. She was brave, always had been, but with the odds so stacked against her and the remaining police force destroyed, she knew it was only a matter of time before they got her too.

The ghouls had made it past the barricade now and they were attacking the news crews. Cameras were knocked aside as the men and women who had been there to record the news now became the news. A woman in a sharp looking blue power suit was brought down and ripped apart, her shrieks filling the air while the camera lying beside her got all the action. Only the newswoman would know if she was pleased that her last seconds on earth were caught in full Technicolor.

Another cop, Christie had graduated the academy with, ran by her and she saw it looked like he was going to make it to freedom, but then two zombies with automatic weapons fired at the man, riddling his body with lead as the cop dropped to the ground. When he fell, his body was only a few feet from Christie's hiding place and she stared at the dead cop's open eyes while blood seeped out of his half-open mouth. Then the body was dragged away by a zombie so it could feed in relative peace.

An explosion ripped through the street and Christie saw one of the squad cars flip onto its side when too many stray rounds found its gas tank. A few zombies and any cops hiding behind the vehicle were caught in the initial blast, their bodies flying ten feet in every direction as they smoldered on the ground. One cop with no face, his eyes burned out from the blast, was crying for help, and when hands grabbed him he thought he was saved. But then the same hands pulled him close, and before he could do anything but utter a shriek, teeth found his charred neck as the zombie decided to see how human meat tasted when it was cooked first.

The staccato of gunshots was dying down now that almost all of the cops were dead and being eaten.

A few more police were still trying to fight off the ghouls, but when ten zombies charged them, soaking up the bullets like they were spitballs, six other ghouls were able to shoot the cops, silencing their return fire forever.

As the cops lay wounded or dead on the ground, the zombies swarmed in and began feeding anew.

Christie decided she needed to leave now or she was going to be joining her fellow police in minutes.

So with a quick look behind her as she hid under the truck, she began crawling out the other side. This side of the barricade wasn't as crowded and she saw she was relatively alone. A few ghouls were off to her right, but they were occupied as they fed on one of the news people.

Moving quickly, she began to run, and it was only as she turned and glanced over her shoulder to make sure she was okay that she spotted something that was odd. She caught all this in a glimpse, but the adage of a picture is worth a thousand words came to mind. She saw another zombie moving through the wreckage, checking to see if any of the cops were still alive. He was tall and wore the standard coveralls of a zombie servant, but that wasn't what caused her to notice him. It was the way he moved. He didn't shamble or hobble. He strode through the area like a conquering general, and in the bright light of the sun, she saw the white streak, like a birthmark, on his dark hair.

Then, as if the ghoul knew he was being watched, his head swiveled and Christie realized the dead man was looking right at her. Their eyes locked together and held for two heartbeats, but then the ghoul raised his hand into the air and pointed at Christie, a guttural yell leaving his cracked lips. In half a second, ten ghouls were jumping to attention and guns were aimed at her. Christie broke from her stupor and began to run just as rounds bounced off the car behind her, shattering glass and peppering the frame with lead. She ran for all she was worth, her arms pumping like she was running a hundred yard dash for track, the prize her life, and soon she was away from the barricade, the SWAT vehicles and other obstructions in between her and the ghouls. The streets were empty, the civilian populace told to stay inside, and as she ran, she wondered where was she supposed to go?

She had no weapon and she was alone. She needed to get to any other remaining police so they could join forces and hopefully stop this madness.

She decided she needed to go to the police station. After all, where else would any other stray police go if they were separated from their units?

So with a burst of speed, she dashed down the sidewalk, while behind her the last remaining screams and gunshots haunted her with their finality.

*   *   *

Jonah was very pleased as he moved through the destruction and death and watched his army feeding. It looked like the victory was complete, and with the exception of the policewoman he had spotted seconds ago, no one had escaped his wrath. All around him were the sounds of feeding as his undead troops ate the cops and soldiers. Some fought like animals for every tidbit while others seemed to share. It was amusing watching this. Even dead it appeared there was some part of their old lives still intact. A selfish man in life was a selfish zombie and so forth.

He turned to his left to see a female ghoul with her left hand stuck down a dead cop's throat. When she pulled her arm back, her hand was filled with the gooey insides from the body. Without hesitation, she began chomping on the bloody gruel, slurping at it like it was barbecue chicken lathered with extra sauce.

Jonah stopped and gazed down at the body of another cop. He leaned over and touched the body and was surprised to hear the man moan.

Ah, good, this one was still alive.

Rolling the man over, he saw there was a large bullet hole in the cop's chest and when he tried to breathe there was a sucking sound coming from the wound, bloody bubbles popping with each intake of breath.

Jonah set his rifle and cattle prod down and stared at the supine man.

"*Help...me...please?*" The soft words bubbled from the dieing man's bloody lips.

Jonah actually smiled then, but the smile did not look reassuring. He knelt down over the man and reached out with his hands. He placed each hand into the man's mouth, one on the upper and one on the lower jaw, like he was going to pull apart a melon with a crack in its center. And that was what he did. As he pulled his arms apart, cracking, ripping, tearing sounds filled the street as the man's jaw was ripped apart like it was a rotten grapefruit.

The head was peeled back from the jaw and the tongue stuck out like a giant slug, the lower half of the jaw now on the man's chest. Blood shot out and Jonah licked it up, the warm liquid revitalizing him. Then he grabbed the upper lip of the severed face and pulled, peeling the flesh from the skull like it was an orange.

With the corpse now ready to be devoured, he leaned down and sunk his teeth onto the flapping tongue, tearing a piece of the soft tissue off as blood squirted into his mouth like he had sunk his teeth into a bloody sponge.

The cop's arms were twitching, his legs spasming as he died a horrible death. Jonah paid it no mind, but reached down to the tongue and tore the rest off with his hand, then began chewing merrily. Behind him, seven ghouls waited. They knew not to intrude on their leader, not until they were told they could. Jonah feasted for another two minutes, chewing happily, and when he was satisfied, he waved his ghouls onward, pointing to the bloody corpse. As one group, the zombies fell on the body as Jonah stepped out of the way. He watched for a few moments as the cop's torso was ripped into, organs torn out to be feasted on, intestines chewed on like sausage links while pancreas and kidney became the juicy delicacy of the day.

Nodding in pleasure, he turned and moved away to inspect the rest of the carnage. While he walked, he continued taking bites out of the slick tongue in his hand, chewing on it like it was a piece of young, tender veal.

When his troops were finished feeding, they would move onward. There was still the rest of the city to destroy and then the entire state.

And if he planned it right, bringing the hundreds of thousands of zombies to his cause, someday very soon he would have the world.

The dead would own the world and the humans would become their prey. That was how it should have happened all those years ago.

Well, he would set things right, and when he was finished, the dead would walk the earth as its masters, not its slaves.

Chapter 9

Marsha slowly came to, pulling herself back to consciousness, and she realized her shoulder hurt. Opening her eyelids a fraction, she saw she was being carried, her left arm draped over the cop's shoulder, her feet dragging behind her.

When he felt her stirring, he stopped and walked over to an empty bench near what was once a bus stop, but had been discontinued when the bus route had been rerouted. The part of town they were in was deserted. So far they had only seen a few other people running past them, their eyes wide with fright. As for any zombies, there had been no sign of them for the past three blocks. Brian was glad. With an empty gun, he felt incredibly vulnerable and was hoping that feeling would go away once he reached the police station. He was confident once there, the rest of the police force would be gearing up for a counterattack and he would be told what to do. He had only been on the force for a year and was still considered a rookie by most. But he knew he could do the job as good as any of the veterans if given the chance.

Marsha moaned and he set her down on the bench, then stepped back to examine her. She seemed okay, but he wasn't a doctor and so didn't know for sure.

"Hey, you all right?"

"What happened?" Marsha groaned.

"Guess you passed out back there. I'm glad you finally came to though. I've been carrying you for six blocks and my back is killing me."

"Are you saying I'm fat?" She asked, looking at him with creased eyes. She was feeling better with every passing second but she was still a little light headed.

"Huh? What, oh no, of course not. I just meant that I had to carry you, is all. No, you're not fat," Brian stammered.

"Whatever," she replied.

"Hey, you got a name? I never got it with all the shit that's happened," Brian said. "I'm Brian by the way. At the moment I think first names are appropriate, don't you?"

"Yeah, I guess so," she muttered. "I'm Marsha."

"Really? Marsha, huh? Like in the Brady Bunch? I used to watch that show all the time. Remember how Janice would always say 'Marsha, Marsha, Marsha,' and then there was the time she got hit with the football. 'Oh, my nose!' she screamed, man I loved that one."

"You're a little young to watch that show, aren't you? I mean, that was on like 30 years ago. And believe me, I've heard them all."

He shrugged. "That's what repeats are for. They're on every day at eleven a.m. I still watch them when I don't have to work," he answered while his eyes studied the street. It looked safe, but that could change at any second. "It must have been nice living way back then, you know, before the plague and all had ever happened."

She didn't answer, her own morbid thoughts coming to her mind.

A gunshot sounded from a nearby street, the echo reverberating off the buildings, and Brian leaned over and grabbed her right arm, pulling her to her feet.

"Hey, let go!" She snapped.

"Can't, they're nearby; we gotta get moving before we're spotted."

Knowing he was telling the truth, she let him pull her along.

"So where are we going anyway?

"The police station, where else? That's where everyone should be who got separated in the attack. And I need more ammo, I'm out. I fired every shot in all four clips I had and I think I only killed three of them. How the hell do you kill them, for Christ's sake? I mean they're dead! But it looks like the head is the best. Take out the brain and they seem to go down and stay down."

"How did this all happen? Why are they attacking us?" Marsha asked in a light voice, as if she was asking herself.

Brian didn't notice and replied.

"I don't know, but whatever did, it's big. There had to be hundreds of them and they had guns, too. I don't think they were taught how to use guns when they got trained to be workers. So if that's so, then who taught them? And who's leading them? They seemed organized as if someone was telling them what to do. I saw them moving in lines and when they were close to us that was when they broke ranks and began tearing into us. I got lucky and when I ran out of ammo I was near the back of the blockade, so I decided there wasn't anything else I could do and I took off. I feel like a coward for doing it, though." He turned to look at her, but she was barely listening. "How the hell am I supposed to face my brothers after ditching them like that?"

She turned to look at him and she could see the angst in his eyes. He was really troubled by what he'd done.

"Look, Brian, right?" He nodded. "Well, Brian, if you hadn't taken off you'd probably be dead too. You had no more bullets; no one will blame you for running. If they do, they're assholes."

He chuckled, smiling a little. "Thanks, that's probably the best pep talk I'm gonna get, so I'll take it.

She grinned back. "Good, that's what it is." Then her face dropped and Brian asked her what was wrong.

"What's wrong? I just realized my two friends are dead. They were torn apart and I would have joined them if it wasn't for you. Thanks, thanks a lot."

He shrugged. "Hey, it's my job, right? To protect and serve."

"Yeah, I guess so," she said.

"Good, now come on," Brian said. "The police station's only a few more blocks that way," he pointed down the street. "Once we're there, everything'll be better, I promise."

With that said he began to jog, wanting to get back as soon as possible. Marsha picked up her pace and the two began making better time as they moved through the empty streets of the city.

*　　*　　*

Brian wasn't able to keep his promise once they reached the police station and the reason was apparent as they entered through the large front doors, the hinges creaking softly thanks to the last maintenance man who would always put the chore off.

The place was a mess of blood and body parts, the walls splashed all the way to the ceiling in crimson; a Pollock painting of blood and guts madly twisted into abstract shapes. Gobbets of flesh hung from every surface and pools of blood congealed in the corners of the floor thanks to the slight slant of the floor.

"Oh my God, what happened in here?" Marsha gasped as she stopped at the doorway. Brian didn't stop, but moved deeper into the police station, stopping at the high desk where the desk sergeant would have been stationed. Now all that was there was a large pile of chewed up organs and blood, the flies already feeding on the clotting liquid. A charnel house odor filled the room and it took all he could do not to gag. Glancing to his right, he saw a blue uniform, or what was left of one. It was torn to shreds, like whoever had been wearing it had been attacked and then consumed by wild animals.

As he stared at the death and blood around him, he felt his legs go weak and he stumbled against the gate leading into the main area of the police station where rows of desks sat like silent soldiers waiting for orders to move out.

"Are you okay?" Marsha asked as she moved forward, catching Brian before he fell.

"Uh, yeah, just dizzy is all," he said, his voice harsh with exhaustion.

Marsha held him up and it was then she noticed he had blood on the side of his shirt, directly under his right armpit. She reached out and gently touched the spot and Brian yelped in pain, wincing, his eyes creasing as he gritted his teeth.

"Have you been shot?" She asked, already knowing the answer.

Breathing hard and fast, Brian nodded. "Yeah, I guess so. It's nothing though, barely hurts," he said stoically.

"Oh, really, then can I touch it again?"

"No!" He screamed, "Don't touch it, why the hell would you do that?"

"To prove a point, Brian. Here, come over here and sit down," she said and directed him through the small gate about waist high. He did as he was told, and soon she had him sitting on a desk, the papers and phone tossed to the floor without care.

"Lie down and let me have a look at your wound," she said, taking charge.

He tried to fight her, telling her he was fine, and she glared at him like a mother to a child.

"I said lay down," she snapped, her tone brooking no argument.

With a subtle nod he did as she instructed, and once prone, she slowly unbuttoned his shirt. His chest was rising and falling and his breath was labored. She realized he had been pushing himself for hours now as he struggled to get them both to the police station, hoping that would be where they would be safe.

When the shirt was undone, she raised the once white t-shirt, the sticky blood making the removal sound like she was peeling scotch tape off of paper. Brain did not yell now, his teeth clamped down hard. Marsha studied the wound, and though she was no doctor, it looked like it was more of a scrape than an actual gun shot. Gingerly, she touched the wound, Brian grunting each time.

"Well, it looks like you got off lucky," she said as she leaned back and gazed down at him.

"Lucky, huh? Shit, if this is lucky I don't wanna know what unlucky is."

"Regardless, you are lucky, Brian. It looks like the bullet only grazed you and then kept going. If you'd been facing the bullet another inch or so it would have gone into your side, but as it is, I think you'll live." She glanced around the station, trying not to look at the blood on the walls for too long. "I need a first aid kit to patch you up."

Brian raised his left hand with a moan and pointed to the rear of the station. "Over there, near the hallway that leads to the cells. There's a first aid kit on the wall."

She said nothing, but patted his chest and then went to get it. As she did, she had to step over pools of blood and organs. A heart lay on its side, the left ventricle chewed up and the obvious signs of teeth marks on it. She pulled her eyes away and kept going. Her nose wrinkled from the smell, but she ignored it. There were worse things in life than the smell of blood and death and she knew she could overcome her distaste if she had to.

So with a sniff and a rub to her nose, she continued to the back of the station. As she walked, she spotted the twelve inch wide white box with the red cross on the wall, just to the right of a dark hallway.

Not thinking twice about just walking over to the first aid kit, she reached out and was about to pluck it from the wall when she heard a noise to her left, coming from the darkened hallway.

Before she had time to react or so much as call out to whoever might be in there, two zombies lunged out of the darkness for her, their hands already prepared to rend her apart.

Marsha had time for one brief squeak of terror, and then she was falling to the floor, the foul stench of rotting flesh filling her sinuses, and as her head struck the wooden floor, she wondered if the last odor she would smell on this earth would be that of the ghouls mixed with her own fear.

Chapter 10

Marsha went down to the floor hard, the back of her head cracking the wood, the impact causing her to see stars. The two zombies were wearing janitorial outfits and wherever they had been before they had decided to stick around the police station after the rest of the undead horde had left.

Their faces and chests were lathered in congealing blood and the miasma of death washed across her face as she tried not to gag.

Quite by accident, she managed to twist her body as she fell, and the first ghoul to attack her was knocked to the side, his body rolling on the floor to come up against a desk. But she still had the other ghoul to deal with, and as she pushed up with shaking arms, yellow teeth snapped only inches from her face. As the zombie tried to bite her, a red and black drool dripped from its mouth, falling onto her forehead. Like a thick gruel it slid down her skin to pool in her ear, causing that side of her hearing to become muffled. She was so scared she knew she was going to wet her pants at any second, but still she fought for her life. A quick glance to her right saw the other ghoul climbing onto its knees to come for her again. As she was occupied with the one on her chest, she knew there would be no stopping the other one from getting her. She could hear Brian calling out to her, but he was across the room and by the time he reached her it would be too late for him to help. No, she was all alone.

The teeth chomped down so close to her nose she felt the air move and she gagged despite herself when some of the brown and yellow drool filled with pus slid into her mouth. It tasted like shit, and she vomited, the warm liquid surging out of her throat to splash the zombie in the face. But what goes up must come down and the bile struck the ghoul's face and then fell back to splash all over her own. She was blind for a few seconds, and when she blinked her eyes clear, she saw two things happening so fast they were like one action.

As the zombie above her moved down to bite her while she was distracted with a face full of vomit, there was a loud crack and the ghoul's head was split in half like a melon. At first she didn't understand what she was witnessing, but then she realized there was the top of a fire axe nestled in the middle of the dead janitor's skull.

The ghoul's hands went wild, spasming uncontrollably, and the legs soon joined them. Then the body went slack, a small geyser of blood escaping from the middle of the sliced head. The axe twisted and the ghoul fell to the side in a heap. Marsha looked up to see a policewoman with dark hair yanking the axe free of the split-open head. Then she heard snarling and turned her head to see the other ghoul was inches from her. But the policewoman was on the attack again and she swung the fire axe like a golf club, using the flat-edged back of it. The thick, heavy metal connected with the ghoul's head and it struck so hard the rotten and decayed neck tissue was no match. Like a large golf ball the head was knocked from the zombie's shoulders at the base of its neck to roll across the floor.

It disappeared under a desk where it was promptly forgotten.

Black ichor that was once blood shot out of the wound to bathe Marsha like a christening of gore. She sputtered and screeched, but there was nothing she could do but take it.

Eventually the fountain subsided and she laid there, her eyes peeking through a face covered in black sludge.

"Hey, you all right?" The policewoman asked. Marsha said nothing, and when she opened her mouth a little, the ichor slid in and she ended up gagging again. Turning her head to the side, she spit up what had come up and tried to regain her composure, which was next to impossible.

"Christie? Is that you?" Brian's voice called as he reached Marsha. He reached down and helped her up as he looked up at the policewoman.

"Brian? Holy crap, thank God; I was beginning to think I was the only one left."

Brian nodded. "You're tellin' me? Look at this place. It's been totaled."

She leaned the axe against the wall and wiped her hands on her pants. She was covered with dirty splotches of red and grime, some on her face. Her once polished shoes were now scuffed and dirty. She looked like she had been through a war and it wasn't that far from the truth.

Marsha was sitting up now and Brian helped her rise. She swayed on unsteady legs and he led her to an office chair. Dropping down, he handed her his police shirt. Using the side not covered in his blood, he wiped her face clean. Marsha said nothing, still a little stunned with her brush with death.

"She gonna be okay?" Christie asked.

"Yeah, I think so. Nice work with the axe," he told her.

She grinned. "Yeah, thanks. I came in through the back and I saw these two deadheads, but I didn't see her," she pointed to Marsha. "If I was only a few seconds quicker I might have saved her from gettin' attacked."

"No worries, you did great," he said. He then became serious. "Weren't you with Sergeant Bronson's unit?"

Her face took on a troubled look as she remembered the slaughter of her unit at the blockade.

"Yeah, I was. That is until we got wiped out." Her voice went soft. "The Sergeant saved me just before he got jumped," she said. Then she looked up. "Hey, have you checked this place out to make sure there aren't any more of these bastards in here?" She pointed to the corpses with her left hand casually.

"No, we just got here ourselves a few minutes before you did," Brian said as he finished wiping Marsha's face. "We can get you cleaned up for real in a few minutes, Marsha. There's a shower in the basement," he told her.

"Thanks, Brian, I think I'd like that," Marsha said as she took his shirt from him. She glanced down at the split-headed ghoul and a chill went down her back. She had come so close to death it was hard to even think about it.

"Hey, Brian, you check the armory yet?" Christie asked. "I lost my gun and I need another one. At the moment I don't think I have to worry about filling out a lost firearm report, though," she added as she moved towards the armory.

"No, as I said, we just got here," Brian said and then winced when he moved. Marsha realized she had never dressed his wound. With something else to deal with other than her own plight, she stood up, wanting to help him and forget her troubles for a few minutes.

"You need to get that wound cleaned and bandaged," she said. "Go lay back down and I'll grab the first aid kit."

"You sure? Don't you want to get cleaned up first?"

"I will, but first you, then a shower would be great," she told him and pushed him to the nearest desk. He nodded, wincing as he walked and picked the closest desk. There were splotches of blood on it but he ignored them, merely laying back down. Marsha grabbed the first aid kit and then went to him. Opening it, she quickly cleaned the wound and applied a bandage.

"There, that should hold you for a while," she said, pleased with herself.

"Thanks, it does feel better," he said and sat up. Just then Christie walked back into the room and she carried a few small pistols and clips.

"There's not much in there. Those bastards cleaned the place out. I only got lucky 'cause I found these in one of the drawers. I guess deadheads don't think about looking in places like that. They just grabbed whatever they could see." She shook her head in disbelief. "I still don't understand how the hell this happened. What could have caused them to revolt like they did? Shit, they're firing guns and eating people. How the hell did they ever figure out how to do that?"

"You're asking me?" Brian said. "I don't know anything more than you do."

Christie nodded. "Yeah, well, I don't know what to say. How the hell are we gonna stop them?"

"You mean just the three of us? That's simple, we can't. We need to find other cops and try to fight back and if this is it, us three I mean, then I think we might want to figure out something else." He moved to the telephone and picked it up. "Just as I thought, it's dead," he said as he placed it back on its receiver. He had a feeling it was true because when he'd entered the station it had been quiet. Usually it was a ringing mess of phones as the people of the city called in for different reasons.

Marsha pointed up at the lights on the ceiling, the fluorescents still humming like worker bees.

"Well, we still have power, do you have a television? Maybe we can see what's going on. The news should be covering this crisis."

Christie laughed. "The news? Hell, sister, the news is the crisis. I saw an entire news crew get attacked and torn apart. Those deadheads don't care who they get. If you're human, then you're a target."

"My name's Marsha, okay? Not sister, and I don't see what it would hurt," she reasoned.

Brian stood up. "She's right, there's a TV in the break room. Christie, you check the street in front of the station and make sure it's clear and I'll go get it. Marsha, why don't you go get cleaned up. There's lockers downstairs and there should be civilian clothes in some of them left by the cops that're out on patrol. I don't think anyone will mind if you borrow a shirt and pants given the circumstances."

"Yeah, all right. This way?" She asked as she moved to the rear of the station.

"Yup, down the hallway where those two deadheads jumped out at you, but there's a door on the left. Take it down to the basement and you'll be fine."

"Hey, Marsha," Christie called to her. "Why don't you wait a second and I'll come with you. In case there's any trouble downstairs."

Marsha nodded. "Okay, I'd like that, thanks."

Christie smiled; a genuine one this time. "No problem, just let me check out front." Then she was weaving through the desks. Marsha stood near the rear of the station and was waiting for Christie to return, and Brian to come back with the TV when she felt something rubbing her toe. At first she didn't give it much thought, but then she glanced down to see the decapitated head of the second ghoul looking up at her. The head was lying on its side and it was trying to bite her sneaker. Its tongue was sticking out as if it could pull her sneaker that one more inch so it could bite her. She screeched and kicked it away, the head rolling away like a soccer ball. It ended up under another desk, but she didn't know which one or care.

Then Christie was back and her eyes were wide.

"You okay? I thought I heard you call out."

Marsha shook her head. "No, I'm fine, thought I saw a mouse."

Christie chuckled. "A mouse, huh? Shit, after everything that's gone down and you're scared of a little mouse?"

Marsha shrugged, "Sorry?"

"Forget it, come on, let's go get you cleaned up, you smell terrible."

Marsha couldn't disagree. She was covered in blood and vomit and the stench was terrible. Christie pulled her newly acquired .38 from her holster and moved down the hallway. When she reached the stairs, she flicked the wall switch for the overhead ceiling lights. They hummed to life and all was silent.

"Looks clear," she said, "let's go."

She began descending the stairs; her police issue boots echoing off the plaster walls while Marsha followed.

As Marsha descended into the basement, she tried to put all the terrible things out of her mind and focus on the shower to come. Maybe when she washed, the water sluicing over her body, she could wash away the terrible memories of the past day, though she highly doubted it would be that easy.

Chapter 11

With Christie in the lead, the two women left the stairwell and stepped out onto the ground floor. The instant Marsha did, the stale odor of sweat and human bodies came to her, but compared to upstairs, the gym locker redolence was a pleasant respite.

Christie waited for a moment, her eyes flicking back and forth in her head as she peered around the small room. There were two doors leading off from where she stood. One was a storage closet and the other would bring them to the showers and locker room where the police officers would change from their street clothes and into their uniforms.

"Hello, anyone down here?" Christie called as she waited for a zombie to pop out. She was prepared to blow it away if that happened, but after more than a minute with still no movement, she decided it was clear.

"Should be okay," she told Marsha. "If there was anything down here it would have come for us, at least that's what I think would happen after seeing what happened upstairs and on the street today."

Marsha nodded, trusting the policewoman; she was anxious to get washed up. Blood had managed to seep past her collar and was now sticking to her lower back, making her sick. Her dress was ruined and her blouse was so filthy the color was almost unknown. All she wanted to do was get out of her rags and get clean. If Christie said the place was clear, that was good enough for her.

"The showers are down there, through that door," Christie said. "You want me to go with you?"

"Why? I'm a big girl, I think I can take a shower by myself," Marsha said back, impatient to go.

"Fine, go, and when you're finished just take what you want from one of the lockers."

Marsha mumbled a curt thanks and moved past Christie, the policewoman watching her go.

"I'm gonna go back upstairs after I wash my face and hands okay?"

"Fine, whatever," Marsha called back dismissively as she stepped through the other doorway and was lost from sight.

"Hmmph," Christie said and walked over to a small sink against the wall, washed up, and then went back upstairs to join Brian. The two needed to do some brainstorming and figure out what they were going to do next.

So with a towel in her hands as she rubbed her face clean, Christie climbed the stairs again, leaving Marsha alone in the showers.

While Marsha turned on one of the showers and steam began filling the air, the warm water splashing the tile floor, blotting out any other sound, the storage room door opened and a shadowy form could be seen as it slowly moved out and into the main room, following the sounds of the shower.

*　　*　　*

Marsha was unaware of anyone else on the floor with her. Christie had left her alone and she was now naked, standing under the warm spray as the water cascaded down her lithe body. As she washed the blood and gore from her hair and face, she cringed when she saw the bruises and scratches on her legs. She knew they would heal, but in the meantime, her once shapely legs looked like a ten-year-old's after a week of climbing trees in shorts.

The water felt incredible, pounding her aching muscles as the heat of the liquid massaged her. She let her worries wash away, and though images continued to haunt her of Robert and Chad being killed, she was also glad she was still alive and knew there would be time to mourn their loss later.

Besides, every survivor of the plague was stronger when it came to personal loss. When most people had lost entire families, the simple death of a friend seemed inconsequential.

With her eyes closed, the water filling her head with its steady beat as it struck the top of her scalp, she never noticed the shadowy form enter the shower area. The steam filled the entire room, and though her skin was turning red from the high temperature, she relished every second of it.

As she rubbed her hair to clean it of debris, the form began to grow clearer and it was only luck that caused her to turn and open her eyes after washing any residue of soap from her hair.

Her eyes went wide as she stared at the pale, wrinkled face of a zombie. It had been a man in life, the once black hair now a mottled gray. The milky-white eyes were bland, and as the dead man opened his mouth, she could see the black tongue lying there like a shriveled worm.

A low moan, not threatening but still there, issued from cracked lips, and she fell backward, wanting to escape the foul creature's touch. For years she had come to take the ghouls as part of life and now she never wanted to see another one.

The ghoul was dressed in the standard gray coveralls of most of its kind, but this one wore an id badge, stating it worked in the police station. On the badge the words **Janitor** were emblazoned in red, and even in her fear induced state, Marsha figured the zombie must have been hiding somewhere when the police station had been ransacked and the officers killed and eaten.

She slipped on the wet tiles and her feet went out from under her, but she turned as she fell and saved herself a crack on the head. Her left arm absorbed the blow, like she had slipped on ice, and she uttered a soft yelp as she gritted her teeth in pain.

The ghoul never slowed, but continued to advance on her, and as she gazed up at it stepping under the hot spray of the shower fixture, she wondered if this was the end.

Water splashed the ghouls head and soaked it through to the bone, and she thought the dead man resembled a water-logged rat.

She knew she was all alone, and if she was going to save herself, she would have to do it on her own, so summoning the courage to fight back, she kicked out with her right foot, her heel connecting with the ghoul's left knee. There was a loud crack, like a tree branch snapping, and the ghoul's leg folded under it like a broken card table leg. It dropped to the tile floor and floundered while water sprayed it in the face. As for Marsha, she was moving, crawling on her hands and knees, ignoring the pain her bare knees felt as she crawled like a baby before it could walk.

Behind her, she could hear the ghoul trying to rise again and her eyes darted every which way at once searching for a weapon. Then her gaze froze on a police issue nightstick lying on a bench from when one of the officers had gone home the previous night. Mindful of the slippery tile, she rose and dashed to the nightstick, grasping for it as water dripped down her face. She felt terribly vulnerable; she was as naked as the day she was born, but she knew there wasn't enough time to be so vain as to get dressed.

With weapon in hand, she spun and on tenuous ground and slid across the wet tiles towards the ghoul. The zombie wasn't able to get up thanks to its shattered knee cap, but it raised it hands to her like a baby wanting to be picked up for a hug.

She ignored the pleas, and with her jaw taut, she brought the nightstick over her head with both hands around the shaft and whacked the ghoul over the head as hard as she could.

As the stick came down, she got another look into the zombie's eyes and she realized this ghoul was like the ones Brian and her had seen on the street as they had made their way to the police station. This ghoul wasn't one of the dangerous ones. It was still domesticated, docile to the point of being helpless, let alone harmless. But though these things flashed in her mind, she also remembered her friends being killed and devoured, and though the ghoul truly posed no threat to her, she took out all of her anger and sorrow on its pitiful form, in many ways mimicking her lost friends when they had beaten the zombie picking up trash.

The nightstick connected to the side of the ghoul's head, just above the temple, and the sick thud overrode the water splashing the tiles. The ghoul went down as if dazed, but it wasn't dead, and in less than a second it was rising again.

"Why don't you die!" She screamed as she brought the nightstick down again, hitting so hard one of the ghoul's eyes was pulverized, the white ooze popping out like a grape was squeezed between a person's fingers. Still she continued; all her anger and fear now focused on this one poor soul who had suffered more than she could ever contemplate. The nightstick went up and down again and again until the zombie's face and skull was nothing but a mottled mess of gore and blood. The water fell from the shower fixture to wash the pus and gore away as fast as it appeared, and the tiles were stained a mute red as the scarlet circles swirled around the drain.

Still Marsha pummeled the ghoul until there was nothing left to recognize. The head was now flat, the white of bone easy to discern thanks to the cleaning from the water. By the time she finished, the water was lukewarm, the water heater exhausted, and she stood over the mangled corpse, her chest heaving, splatters of blood covering her from head to toe. Wiping her forehead clear of blood, she smeared it across her face more and she looked like a crazed killer after massacring a family who had been asleep in their beds.

As she stared down on the prone form, the head nothing but mush, her shoulders began to shake, and before she could stop herself, she began to cry, rich heavy sobs that wracked her body. Her tears were lost in the spray of water and she leaned against the wall, sliding down to the floor as the water still fell to wash the ghoul clean.

She didn't know how long she cried, but it couldn't have been too long, and when she had sobbed out all of her angst and fear, she stood up. Turning on the next shower fixture, she washed yet again, now rinsing the blood of what could be considered an innocent off her body, and when she was through, she stepped out of the shower area and began to towel off. The nightstick lay where she had dropped it, the tip now clean of blood thanks to the shower.

Though she felt exhausted and drained, in many ways she felt cleansed, and after finding some clothes that fit her in one of the metal lockers, she slid into the pants and shirt and brushed her hair with a brush found the same way.

She kept her sneakers, as they weren't that bad, and when she felt as composed as she could manage given the circumstances, she left the shower area and headed back upstairs, the corpse left where it had fallen. As she left, the water now off, the only sound was the soft drip, drip, of the shower fixture as the tiny drops fell to land on the mangled face of the dead janitor.

Chapter 12

Near the middle of the city, Jonah was in a state of all out war with his undead followers.

The army had arrived and had set up a sweeping perimeter around his growing horde of undead, for the moment not firing, but trying to keep him and his undead horde contained.

But in the time it had taken the military to get into position, Jonah's undead army had grown exponentially and there were far too many for the humans to stop. He now had more than five hundred bodies following him, the zombies all in different states of intelligence.

The freshest ones to be shocked by cattle prods were in the lead as they were able to formulate ideas, and near the back of his army were the ones who had been with him the longest; their dull brains now only able to think of two things, to kill and to eat.

Jonah glanced at the buildings on either side of him, and he spotted a restaurant, the bright red sign and straight-edged facade of the place causing him to have memories of when he was human. He remembered being here with Marsha, his fiancée, the two of them having a quiet dinner together. This was where he had proposed to her and she had been so happy she'd cried.

They had gotten champagne, and after finishing their meal and the bottle, had returned to his apartment and had made love for the entire night.

Shaking these images from his mind, he realized they were worthless now. Who he had been when he was alive was not who he was now.

Now he was dead, a creature trapped between life and death and though he didn't want to admit it, all he had left was revenge.

Revenge on the people who had made him this way; had pulled him back from the peace of death to make him their slave.

All around him the dead milled about, waiting for the orders to attack.

Jonah was off to the side, now smart enough to never be in the spear head of any attack on the humans. His sense of survival was too strong now and he knew what a bullet could do to his frail, rotting body.

In front of him and the rest of his army was yet another blockade, large green trucks with canvas flaps parked at odd angles on the street. Soldiers with rifles stood in front of the trucks, some on their knees, while others stood behind them.

There was a man decked out with medals to the side, a two-way radio in his hand as he spoke into it, giving orders to his men.

There were a few Hummers scattered about and even an M-60, set up on one of the trucks. This was going to be the fight of his unlife, Jonah realized, as he stared at the humans.

He glanced behind him, seeing his undead army shifting about. More than half had firearms, taken from the police station, dead cops, and other soldiers. The rest held weapons of all sizes and shapes. Many welded large blades, machetes, steak knives and cleavers, to name a few.

For the first two minutes, when Jonah stopped his army, the soldiers did nothing, but stared at the wall of dead flesh before them.

Then one nervous soldier, scared out of his wits, fired into the undead crowd, which then began a chain reaction of shooting. Jonah growled high and loud, waving for his walking dead to attack, and in seconds the wails of the dead filled the street. The ghouls charged forward like they were attacking the beach at Normandy and the first wave was gunned down by a fusillade of hot lead, but as they went down, the next wave climbed over them, soaking up bullets and shrugging them off. The soldiers weren't shooting for heads, they were treating the zombies like any other human attackers and that was their downfall. While arms and legs were blown off by the scores, still dozens made it to the perimeter of the soldier's blockade and swarmed in between the men. Like before, the soldiers began shooting at the ghouls and ended up shooting one another. One soldier held a grenade, the pin pulled, and prepared to toss it into a large knot of animated walkers, but before he could toss it, a machete wearing zombie came at him and lopped off his arm. The grenade fell to the ground, the hand still clutched around it, and a second later the grenade exploded. The zombie and the one armed soldier were blown to Hell, their body parts raining down on the other fighters. Another soldier shot round after round into the bodies coming at him, and though his gun barrel became red hot, he never managed to stop the assault. As he fired the last round in his clip, a ghoul lunged for him and stabbed him in the heart with a long steak knife. The soldier barely managed a scream before his breath was sucked away and he sagged to the ground, dead. The ghoul fell on top of the body and began tearing into it, ripping the green uniform off as it dove in for the warm flesh beneath.

The hundreds of rounds being discharged ignited a car parked against the curb and it exploded in a raging fireball of orange and yellows. More than thirty ghouls were caught in the blast and the walking torches flailed their hands in the air as their eyeballs melted and their rotting flesh peeled and cracked as it burned and melted like wax paper. Red muscled tissue could be seen peeking through the cracked flesh as the top layers of skin were burnt away to fall to the pavement like ash. Hair dissolved in seconds as the ghouls stumbled around blind, sometimes attacking each other, but other times still reaching the soldiers where they began to pull them to the ground. They didn't need eyes to kill and they proved it again and again. But more than half caught in the blast were burned to the point of dying for good, their brains boiling in their skulls and their skin turned to blackened ash.

As they fell to the street to curl up into fetal positions, their muscles contracting from the heat as bones cracked, the rest carried onward, their goal the eradication of the soldiers

The man with the medals, a colonel or captain, perhaps, continued screaming into his radio for his men to defend themselves. On the back of one of the trucks, the M-60 roared, spraying the wall of flesh and chopping the bodies into thick gobbets of blood and pus. But there were more undead coming and the soldiers were losing at every turn. The zombies knew no fear while the soldiers didn't want to die and that was the edge the living dead needed to win the day.

As the gunner with the M-60 riddled bodies with tracers, he didn't see more ghouls coming up on him from behind. Before he realized what was happening, five zombies reached up and yanked him off his perch by his uniform, the M-60 going silent.

But it didn't remain that way for long. One ghoul, who still had his wits about him, climbed up and turned the massive weapon on its owners; chopping the soldiers to warm pieces of flesh which the zombies quickly fell upon with gusto.

The man with the medals screamed again into his radio and then turned at the sound of battle directly behind him. His three guards were shooting at the ghouls who were even now charging for them, but they only shot them in the chest. Absorbing the impacts, the zombies lunged for the men and quickly took them down, taking their weapons from them and shooting each soldier in the chest, killing them instantly.

"You bastards! You have no right! You're dead!" The man with the medals screamed.

The ghouls could have cared less what the man said. Swinging rifle barrels around, the man with the medals was shot off his feet to fall into a crowd of ravenous ghouls. As he gasped his last breath, he felt yellow nails and brown teeth ripping into his flesh. Then he knew no more.

Jonah stood to the side watching the carnage with pride.

It had taken less than ten minutes, but the street was his. All the soldiers were dead, his army feeding on their twitching corpses. Strolling into the chaos, he reached down and plucked a bloody kidney from a dead soldier. Biting into it, feeling the warm liquid slide down his throat, he felt strength filling him.

Nothing could stop him or his undead army, and soon he would gather even more, and with thousands behind him, he would swarm over the rest of the state and then the country until the entire United States was a continent of the dead.

Managing a grin, he began gathering some of the more intelligent ghouls to him, instructing them with hand signals and grunts to gather the horde.

There were many more humans to kill before the darkness fell and he didn't want to keep them waiting any longer than he had to.

In time, he gathered his army and they moved out, leaving the remnants of the smoking, charred and dismembered corpses behind to rot in the sun.

Jonah had no doubt that somewhere in the abyss, the entity known as Death was laughing.

Thanks to Jonah, there was no doubt Death would be filling his quota today.

Chapter 13

Upon leaving the stairwell and stepping out onto the ground floor of the police station, Marsha saw Christie and Brian near the front, a small television set propped on a desk. Both were watching intently and didn't see her until she was only a few feet away.

Christie was the first to glance up and she gave her a wan smile.

"Hey, how was your shower?"

"Fine, it was fine," Marsha said, not mentioning the ghoul she'd had to kill. After all, what would be the point? "What're you guys watching?"

"The news," Brian started blandly. "There's a massive crowd of deadheads attacking a military blockade a quarter mile from here and it doesn't look good for our team."

"Our team?" Marsha asked.

"Yeah, the living, our team. Us against them, the living against the dead."

She only nodded and moved closer so she could see the screen better. It was grainy and black and white, the bent rabbit ears on top proclaiming just how old the set was. And perhaps that was a good thing. As she watched the screen, she saw the small forms running and jumping slowly at each other, the undead not able to move that fast. Soldiers were shooting at the hundreds of bodies, but though they were shot down, there always seemed to be more to take their place. Then a car went up in a blazing grey fireball, thanks to the lack of color on the screen, and dozens of bodies began to burn.

All three of them looked up as the building itself shook slightly from the same car blast only a few streets over.

"Shit, that was close," Brian said. "That sounded like it came from the center of city."

"Probably the north end of Broadway?" Christie suggested.

Brian nodded. "Yeah, suppose so." He glanced at each woman's face while he was thinking and then he slapped his hand down on the desk. "Look, guys, I don't think we can stay here. Whatever the hell is going on in this city, it doesn't look good for anyone living. I think we need to try and get out of the city, maybe see if we can get some transportation and head south. Once we're away from all this maybe we can get a message to the State Police or something."

"Why bother?" Christie asked. "If the military is here then surely they know what's happening," she stated as she watched the small grey blobs of burning things move about the television screen. It was like she was watching an old horror movie from when she was a kid, the dead somehow rising to attack the living.

"Maybe and maybe not," Brian said. "I think those boys in green are local, from the next town over. It's possible this shit hasn't gone beyond the city limits. Besides, don't you think it's our duty to make sure? We are cops after all."

"Yes, Brian, I'm fully aware of our responsibilities," Christie said wryly, "but I also don't want to end up like the rest of our police force, dead and ripped to pieces."

He couldn't argue with that. It seemed at the moment they might be the only two police left in the city and that did not bode well for the city at all.

"Maybe so, but we still have to try. If not for us then what's left of our families and friends."

"He's right, Christie," Marsha spoke up. "I don't have anyone left but an aunt but I know I don't want her to get killed. We need to at least make sure the proper authorities know what's happening here. It's very possible Brian's right, and with the exception of the small military base outside the city, no one else knows what's happening. As farfetched as that seems. But maybe they don't want anyone else to know what's going on here, ever think of that?"

"Oh, great, a conspiracy theory, are you one of those nuts?"

Marsha shook here head no. "No, not really, but I am a realist."

But what about the news?" Christie asked. "They're broadcasting live and other cities will see it, too," she said as she gestured to the set. The undead forms on the TV were now swarming over the soldiers and the camera was getting it all.

Brian shook his head. "I doubt it, Christie, this is local TV only. It doesn't go that far outside the city, just the few surrounding towns. But you know as well as I do there's no one there anymore. Ever since the plague, those towns are pretty much empty. And most of them still don't have phone service. Hell, they just got electricity a year ago. In case you haven't noticed, there's no one left to hang the wires."

Christie crossed her arms in annoyance. "I'm well aware of that, thank you, wiseass," she mumbled as she turned away to walk around the desk.

"Guys, come on, don't fight, you both make good points," Marsha said, trying to keep the peace.

"Oh, shit, will you look at that?" Brian said as pointed back to the black and white screen.

On the television, the ghouls had now totally overwhelmed the soldiers and had continued on to the news crew. The anchor and camera man were attacked and forced to the ground, the picture spinning as the camera toppled to the ground to lie on its side. From this vantage point everything was sideways, but they could still watch in horror as the ghouls took down the camera man and anchor, as well as the technicians, and began ripping into them, a few zombies shooting any humans trying to escape. Before the signal was lost for good, the screams of the news crew added to the melee, gunshots and shrieks of pain the song of the day.

Before the camera went dark forever, they watched a newsman get shot in the chest, and as the man fell back to the street, bodies swarmed over him and ripped open his insides. One man, a large fat guy with two hundred pounds of blubber, was ripped open and layers of thick, greasy fat resembling gray cottage cheese was exposed as the ghouls tore it from his voluminous body and then dug into the tender organs within. Some didn't care and ate the fat in huge handfuls, the small circles of fat sliding out between their fingers. It was highly doubtful these ghouls were worried about their cholesterol as they gorged themselves on the fat man's cellulite.

Then the screen went dark for good, the sound hanging on for a few seconds longer before fading away, the screams filling the police station before all was silent.

Brian got up and tried another channel, but all he got was a test symbol over and over again.

"There's no other channels on. What the fuck?"

"Christ, did you see that? They tore that guy to pieces," Christie said as she replayed the visceral scene in her head.

"What does this all mean? What's gonna happen to us?" Marsha asked, her voice shaky with fear.

Brian turned the useless set off and spun around to glare at both women.

"It means if we don't get the fuck out of this city we're gonna be joining those poor bastards real soon."

As if to illustrate his point, an explosion from a nearby street shook the police station to its very foundation and the overhead lights blinked out, casting them in darkness.

No one spoke, there was nothing to be said. The ominous darkness cast a pall of doom over them all as each contemplated their coming fate.

Christie turned and began walking away, Brian calling after her.

"Where're you going," he asked.

She stopped. "To the bathroom, I need a few minutes alone, all right?"

He nodded, Marsha only staring at her. Christie turned then and moved away, her slim form soon swallowed by the darkness now permeating the station. Only a few thin stray beams of light were able to penetrate along the sides where the white washed windows were set.

Marsha leaned against a desk and sighed heavily, the day finally catching up to her. She thought back to only a few minutes ago when she had been caught off guard in the showers and she realized she had pummeled that ghoul into mush. Before she realized it, she began sobbing, letting all of her emotions free as she cried in the dark. Not knowing what to do, Brian moved next to her, Marsha not seeing him, her eyes closed as she cried. He raised his hand and held it an inch from her shoulder, wanting to console her, touch her, but at the same time wondering if he was overstepping himself. For all he knew, if he touched her she would become upset or enraged and he didn't want that. Women were a funny creature, he knew from experience.

But the more she sobbed, the more his heart went out to her, and eventually he let his instincts take over and he lowered his hand onto her shoulder, squeezing gently. She slowed her crying and reached up with a hand, holding his under hers.

Neither spoke, Brian not knowing what to say and Marsha not feeling the need for words. As he stood there, his hand on her shoulder, he moved closer until his body was only a few inches from hers. Before he knew what was happening, she shifted position and fell into his arms, her head lying against his chest. Without thinking, he did what felt natural when someone embraces you and he wrapped his arms around her, hugging her tightly. Immediately, he could smell the sweet scent of her hair and feel how soft she was.

The two of them remained still, two bodies becoming one in the middle of the gloom of the police station, holding one another and taking solace in each other's company, knowing they were there with whatever moral support they could give.

This went on for almost five minutes and they only separated when Christie's footsteps could be heard as she approached them from the rear of the station. As she approached, they separated, but looked into each others eyes with a new sense of discovery. For the first time since she had met him, Marsha realized Brian was a handsome man, with strong features and dark brown hair with a few curls at the top. His deep green eyes and strong chin gave him a Hollywood leading man look, though he was only in his twenties. As she held him close, she felt his arms, the tendons and muscles honed from years of working out and staying in shape.

Then Christie was with them again and the mood was broken.

"So, when are we gonna go?" She asked as she picked a seat on a desk near them. She shoved the papers on the desk to the side, not caring about them in the least.

Brian turned to look at her, his face shrouded in shadows. "I say we leave first thing in the morning. You saw that shit on the TV; it's pretty bad out there right now. Hopefully, by tomorrow morning we can take one of the squad cars from the motor pool and get the hell out of Dodge."

Christie nodded, the gesture barely seen.

"Sounds good, well, I don't know about you guys but I'm starving," she said as she rose to her feet.

For the first time since being at the fast food restaurant hours ago, Marsha realized she was hungry, too.

"What've you got?" Marsha inquired.

Christie gestured to the rear of the station, in the same room where the TV had been, which was the break room for the cops.

"There's a few vending machines back there, we should be able to get enough to eat."

Brian clapped his hands in anticipation. "Sounds good, so let's go," he said, but then he stopped, walked over to the main doors and slid the bolt, locking the doors.

"What'd you do that for?" Christie asked.

"Simple, if anyone comes, they can bang on the door, but until then I'm not taking any chances." He patted his Glock, now with a full clip thanks to what Christie had found. "Whatever's happening right now out there we need to be smart. The second we get careless we're dead, agreed?"

"Agreed," Christie replied, Marsha nodding, too. It was times like this when she felt out of place with the two cops. They shared a comradery she knew nothing about.

With the main doors locked, and the station secured, Brian led them to the break room for some much needed food, while outside in the neighboring streets, the city crumbled a little more with each passing second.

Chapter 14

A little more than an hour later, while Christie and Brian were in the armory of the police station, going over what they had for ammunition and weapons, Marsha sat quietly in the desk sergeant's chair, gazing out through the windows of the front doors. The street was dark now, the sun just setting, and the only illumination was from the sparse stars and a sliver of the moon peering from behind the clouds.

She held a pencil in her right hand and tapped it lazily on the desk, her other hand supporting her chin as she stared out into nothing.

So at first she didn't think she'd heard the soft cries for help that permeated the thick wooden doors. At first she had continued gazing into the night, but then she heard it again, the distinct cries of a human voice.

Her head perked up and she began looking around the police station, as if a policeman would pop up and tell her he was going to check it out, but of course there was no one. The station was all but darkness, only the small amount of light from a flashlight where the two cops were working in back.

Marsha sat taller in her chair, her mind racing with what she should do, when the cries grew louder. They couldn't be more than a dozen car lengths away from the station.

Standing up, she looked to the back, figuring she should go tell Brian what was happening, but when the cries continued she decided to investigate herself, not wanting to be the damsel in distress who always needed to run to someone else for help. It was a stubborn trait she'd always had and she didn't give it a second's thought as she moved around the desk to the main doors.

Absently, the pencil was still in her hand while she unlocked the door and snuck a peek outside. The street was deserted and silent, though over the buildings directly across from her she could see the orange and yellows of fires burning, and the odor of smoke came to her tongue. There were fires burning with no one to put them out. A few gunshots could be heard; echoing in the street like it was a large canyon, bouncing off the facades of the surrounding structures. But they were far away, thank God.

Sliding out the door, she looked back and forth, wondering if she had imagined what she'd heard when another cry for help came to her ears, sounding like it was coming from her right.

Descending the stairs, she stepped onto the sidewalk and began moving forward towards the cries, though a slight hesitation filled her. Maybe she should go get Brian and Christie. After all, they have guns; they could protect themselves.

Besides, what could she do to help someone?

She was turning to go back inside and do just that when a high-pitched scream filled the street and Marsha spun back around. Whoever was calling out needed her now or it sounded like by the time she got Brian it would be too late.

She began walking faster, the pencil still tightly gripped in her hand as she followed the sidewalk until she was two buildings over from the police station. There was an alley between the two buildings, a few trash cans, overflowing with rubbish to the side, and the end of the alley was wreathed in darkness.

Then another scream, this one more muffled, came out of the alley and she knew she'd found the origination of the disturbance.

"Hello, are you all right?" She called into the darkness, already realizing this was a really bad idea.

She heard movement and a hushed voice coming from somewhere in that obsidian, inky blackness and she was already beginning to back away from the alley, deciding she needed to get Brian, when footsteps could be heard coming towards her. Then a man appeared out of the alleyway and wrapped a large, hairy hand around her thin wrist.

"Come 'ere, bitch, we wanna talk to ya," the man growled, his breath smelling of stale beer and old cigarettes.

Before Marsha could do anything, she was yanked off her feet and was being dragged into the alleyway like she was a small girl being led by an angry father.

The hand on her wrist squeezed like a vise and she bit her lip in pain, but she didn't scream, at least not yet. In seconds she was in the alleyway and now saw who had been crying out in pain. There was another woman on the ground, her clothing torn off and in rags beside her. On top of her was another man, and as his butt cheeks moved up and down in a steady rhythm, it was apparent he was in the act of fornication. The woman on the ground was crying, but she couldn't scream thanks to the man's hand over her mouth. Each time he slammed himself into her, she would moan, her head moving an inch upward only to slide back down as the man withdrew from her.

She was being raped and Marsha realized she was about to join the woman she had come to help.

Before Marsha could yell out, a meaty fist slammed into her jaw, causing her to see stars in the darkness. But the man still held her wrist so she didn't go far. She fell away from the punch, but was then yanked back, like she was on a bungee cord, the man now wrapping his arms around her as he began kissing her neck, cheeks, then her mouth. He slid his tongue between her clamped lips and she wanted to gag, the foul taste of cigarettes and beer filling her with sickness. The man then pulled his head away and grabbed her hair, pulling it back.

"Better be nice to me, bitch, or I can make it a whole lot harder," he growled as he began removing her clothing.

At first Marsha was in a state of shock, but slowly she regained what little she had of her senses and realized she needed to escape this man or she was in for a world of pain.

As the man ripped open her shirt, she saw her chance and kicked up with her left foot, feeling the soft testicles between the man's thighs deflate, followed by a groan of pain as he bent over. She spun, wanting to run away, but the man reached out and grabbed a handful of her hair, pulling back and causing her to scream. She was fairly certain some of her hair had been pulled out by the roots, he'd tugged so hard. Like a dog on a leash, she was pulled backward and thrown hard onto her back. The man never let go of her hair and her head turned sharply as her body landed in the filth-encrusted alley.

"Oh, you're gonna pay for that, bitch," he breathed, wheezing in pain as he moved to get on top of her, one of his hands already reaching down for the unfastening of her pants.

"Come on, man, just fuck her already," the other rapist hissed as he pumped harder. The trapped woman below him managed to bite the hand over her mouth and he yelped in pain as he pulled it away, then he took both palms and wrapped them around the suffering woman's neck, squeezing the life out of her as he pumped like never before. Even in the darkness, the woman's face began to turn blue, her eyes bulging from her head like they were a child's toy.

"What the fuck do ya think I'm tryin' ta do?" Marsha's attacker hissed back as he fumbled with her pants. He was breathing heavily now and she figured she had only dealt him a glancing blow between the legs.

It was as he began to pull down her pants that she remembered she still had the pencil in her hand. Thinking she still had a chance, she now waited, gauging the right time to try and save herself. She cringed when her panties were pulled down to her ankles, the man not even bothering to take them off, and it was when he crawled on top of her, his face only a few inches from hers in the darkness, that she chose to strike, her hand darting forward in the blackness to find his left eye.

The tip of the pencil struck the orb dead center, piercing the pupil and then sliding deeper, more than two inches. The man screamed long and loud, then rolled off her, Marsha scrambling away, while behind her chaos reigned. The first man who had been on top of the other woman stopped what he was doing and went to his friend's aid, while Marsha crawled on hands and knees to escape them. The man had a hand to his eye, and when she turned to see if they were following, on a sliver of light cast in the alley she saw the illuminated man reach up and pull the pencil from his eye socket, the eye coming out with it, now impaled on the pencil like it was the beginnings of a shish-kebab. The former rapist screamed long and loud as tendrils of pink viscera dropped from his eye socket. His other eye was open wide, filled with pain and anger, and it locked onto Marsha's scurrying form as she tried to reach the end of the alley.

"You bitch, you fucking bitch, I'm gonna kill you!" He roared as he tossed the pencil and orb to the ground and began to run at her, his thick legs making him charge forward like a bull.

Marsha tried to get up and run, but the terror inside her was too much. Her feet slipped on the slime in the alley and she knew she was never going to make it. And even if she did, what would happen then? The man would simply get her on the deserted street and drag her back into the alley to finish what he'd started, only this time with much more pain and suffering added to the mix.

With trembling limbs, Marsha tried to escape, but she knew there would be no freedom this time. The first time when Brian had appeared had been a miracle, he had saved her from certain death, but this time her luck had run out.

As the man towered over her, and was reaching down to grab her by her golden tresses yet again, she wondered how she could have been so foolish as to venture out of the police station alone.

Then another shape appeared at the end of the alley, and as the rapist reached down to grab her, there was the loud report of gunshots and a flash of light as each round found its chosen target.

The rapist was thrown backward, reaching for his already bloody chest as dark spots of blood splattered the alley walls.

Then a flashlight was turned on and the rapist was caught in the beam, his face a mask of rage and shock as he stared at the bullet holes in his chest. But the man wasn't down. Whether it was because of his large mass or perhaps he was high on something, he roared with rage and began charging at the flashlight. Behind the light, Marsha could see nothing, her eyes now blinded by the glare.

Three more shots rang out and this time the rapist was thrown backwards, one shot catching the man in the temple. The head snapped back and the arms went wide as the body dropped to the alleyway, dead.

The flashlight shifted from the man to Marsha, then went deeper into the alleyway. Marsha followed the beam and saw the back of the other rapist as he dashed out the opposite side of the alley, his pants still down by his ankles, the woman he'd been assaulting lying still on the ground.

The figure holding the flashlight held his fire, knowing the other rapist was already too far away to bother trying to shoot, then the light beam was aimed down to the ground to diffuse its beam, and in the illumination, Marsha saw it was Brian.

He went to her, kneeling down beside her, his face a mask of concern.

"You all right? I came out from the armory and you were gone, and the front door was open, then I heard someone cry out. What the hell happened here?" Though he had a pretty good idea anyway.

She gathered her words before speaking, not wanting her voice to crack, and then she filled him in on what she'd heard and how she had gone to investigate.

Brian leaned back on his haunches, his eyes wide with disbelief.

"Jesus, Marsha, that was reckless of you. You could have gotten killed out here. How the hell did you know what you might find?"

She nodded. "Yeah, I know that now. I was about to come back and get you when he grabbed me and pulled me into the alley," she said while gesturing to the dead rapist.

Brian only nodded. "Well, you're safe now, I'm just glad I got here when I did," he said as he helped her to stand.

"You and me both," she added. Then her eyes went wide. "Oh, wait, there's another woman down there, we need to help her," she said and began running into the darkness while she pulled up her pants.

"Marsha wait, don't go down there yet…" Brian tried to stop her, but she was already on the move. Shaking his head at her recklessness, he followed her, his flashlight playing over the walls of the alley, checking anyplace someone could be hiding. His beam stopped when it reached the dead rapist and he saw the missing eye, blood seeping down from the gaping socket. He saw the chest of the corpse was a mess of torn flesh thanks to his shots and he nodded, pleased with himself. No man knew how he would act under pressure when the actual time came and he was proud of himself. He had acted accordingly. Plus, he doubted if there would be a righteous shoot inquiry happening anytime soon, not with what was happening in the city.

Moving the beam of the light towards Marsha, he saw she was already leaning over the still form of the other woman. When he moved closer still, he could see the prone woman wasn't moving, not so much as a finger twitching.

When he was next to her, Marsha moved to the side and looked up at him.

"I think she's dead," she said softly.

Brian kneeled down, turning the flashlight to the side so as not to be blinded by the light and touched the woman's neck, searching for a pulse. As he did this he stared into her open eyes and saw nothing there that would signify she was still alive. He took his hand away from her neck, finding no pulse, and saw in the flashlight beam the red marks on her throat where her rapist had squeezed the life from her, strangling her even as he assaulted her.

"She's dead, Marsha, sorry to say, we're too late for her."

"But how? She was alive a minute ago, she can't be…"

"Afraid so, looks like she was strangled. The bastard, I wish I had taken a shot at him, If I'd known he'd done this I would have," Brian said as he stood up, shaking his head in disgust. With so much happening in the city there were still humans who would prey on other humans, taking the opportunity to hurt one another.

"Come on, let's get back to the station, there's nothing we can do for her now."

"But we can't just leave her like this? It's disrespectful," Marsha said as she was lifted to her feet by Brian.

Brian had to agree with her, but there was nothing they could do for the poor woman now. Then he spotted a large cardboard box to the side of the body and went to it, ripped it open so it could be laid flat, then he gently set it in top of the woman like a makeshift shroud.

"There, that's about it, I'm sorry to say. Come on, we need to go. It's not safe out here."

Marsha gazed down at the cardboard box, thinking it could have been her under there, as well, her body left to rot in the filthy alley after being violated, and it made her want to cry. But she held it back, not wanting to cry yet again in front of Brian. She had always thought she was a strong woman, but after the past day she truly wondered just how strong she really was.

Brian led her out of the alley and back onto the street. A few more gunshots could be heard echoing in the distance which was then followed by a loud explosion. They both turned west to see a blossoming mushroom cloud of yellows and reds rolling into the sky, which then slowly subsided to a dull glow.

"That must have been the gas station on 5th Street, I'd bet," Brian said as he watched the flames lick the sky, then he began walking again. "This shit is getting real bad, Marsha, I hope we can get out in one piece tomorrow."

Marsha didn't reply, still thinking of the dead woman in the alleyway.

As the two people moved away from the alley and walked down the street, another form appeared in the darkness from the opposite end.

A ghoul stumbled out of the shadows, attracted to the screams and gunshots of only moments ago, and stood over the supine body. The zombie reached down, pulling the cardboard off the corpse like it was unwrapping a TV dinner. This ghoul had been separated from the main group of undead lead by Jonah and had gone in search of food on its own.

Its intelligence was nearly gone now, only the will to feed still remaining. Kneeling over the prone body of the woman, it began feeding, tearing at the exposed flesh with blackened teeth. The corpse was still warm and the ghoul fed well, tearing open the chest cavity and cracking the ribs like a starving man eating a roast chicken.

By the time the zombie was finished, its stomach was bloated to the point of bursting thanks to half the woman's insides now in its gut.

Then, after picking a few choice, bloody chunks of meat for the road, the ghoul stood up and stumbled out of the alley, wandering away like a drunk after last call.

No sooner was the zombie gone then rats appeared from under boxes of trash and debris. Their noses twitched in the darkness as they scanned the area to make sure all signs of man were gone. When confident they were truly alone, the furry creatures darted out and began feeding on the corpse.

The circle of life continued no matter what had died.

Meat was meat and the rodents were hungry.

Chapter 15

Jonah had the same problem the leaders of armies have had since the dawn of warfare.

How to keep his men fed.

And he had come up with a solution to this dilemma.

Where before he had a thirst for revenge, wanting to wipe out every human he found, now he realized there was a better use for them.

For the past half a day he'd been gathering all the humans in the city he could find, and instead of killing them, his undead horde had been capturing them and taking them to a large warehouse along the water front, near the city docks.

Of course there were always a few ghouls who simply couldn't follow orders and would end up tearing apart the humans where they found them, but for the most part his dominion over his army was strong enough for them to resist the urge to kill, if only by a miniscule amount.

It seemed once the undead had a taste for human flesh, they couldn't stop eating. Jonah couldn't blame them very much. Soon as he had begun feeding on the living he had never felt so alive, so to speak. And his body appeared stronger, the frailness now giving way to muscle tone. It seemed with the consummation of the blood and flesh of the living, the dead were able to regenerate partly, like how a human would heal after receiving a bad cut. Of course, missing limbs and eyes couldn't be grown back, but the undead digestive systems were somehow able to use the flesh and plasma to make them stronger. Even when he was alive, Jonah was never much for the details of things. The fact that it was true was enough for him and he would leave the idiots to debate science until the end of time.

The warehouse was a massive structure of steel and metal, with only one section set aside for offices. There was a large steel staircase that led to these offices and it was here that Jonah had set up his command post. Even now, as he gazed out the dirty plate-glass window of the front office down to the warehouse below, he felt something he thought he would never feel again.

Pride.

Below on the ground floor, trapped in cages or just encircled by his minions, almost all of the living humans left in the city were secured. Now, as they set off to take over more cities and states, they could bring the humans with them and feed on them when need be. It was the equivalent of taking his food supplies along on the journey.

The sun had set in the sky and by morning he would be setting off for the next town. A map on the desk in the office told him he had to walk more than ten miles, but when you were dead, distance meant nothing.

He walked away from the window and went to the door, opened it, and stepped out onto the small metal balcony, the stairs leading down to his right. All eyes went to him, human and undead alike as he gazed down on his kingdom.

It was hard to believe less than a day ago he was a simple slave and now he ruled an army of the dead.

He raised his left hand high and then pointed to a woman in one of the cages with thirty other terrified humans. Immediately, the undead turned and went for her, the woman's husband trying to fend them off, but he was overwhelmed and separated from her. The woman cried tears of fear as she was dragged away and out of the cage to be knocked to the floor. Her eyes were wide with terror as she stared at the undead faces glaring down at her and she whimpered and cried for someone to help her, but there was no one. If ever a human being had no hope of survival, of knowing in a matter of a minute they would be dead, it was this woman.

As for the other humans, they did nothing, merely cowered in fear and thanked God it wasn't them being picked.

The woman was dragged to the middle of the warehouse and surrounded by more than fifty ghouls, and when Jonah lowered his hand, his thumb pointing downward, the woman was set upon by a dozen hands, her clothing ripped from her shaking frame. When her clothing was off and she was bare to the world, Jonah raised his thumb up again and ten ghouls set upon the woman, nails and teeth tearing her to red, bloody ribbons. Each ghoul took a piece and then stepped back as others moved in for their turn. Her rib cage was cracked open and each rib was ripped from her heaving chest as the ghouls began feeding. Organs were dug from her chest cavity as she gasped in pain, eventually expiring with eyes still open and mouth gaping wide. She actually lived for a very long time until her heart was ripped from her body, the organ still beating a few more paltry thumps before stopping when yellow teeth chomped into the muscle, hot blood squirting out to splatter any nearby faces.

Her open mouth was invaded when a ghoul went in and shoved a hand down her throat, going for the tongue and ripping it out, biting into the pink morsel with gusto.

By the time all fifty ghouls had taken a piece of the woman, there was nothing left of her but blood-red cement and a few gobbets of torn flesh. As for the woman, she was now distributed amongst this undead army, some feasting on her legs and arms like they were massive turkey legs.

Jonah nodded, pleased with the control of the ghouls. Hopefully, in time, they would be able to control their blood lust so they could maintain their supply of humans indefinitely. And he had already begun making plans for setting aside humans as breeders, then they could raise children which would feed his army forever. The key was not to be greedy. If they killed every human then there would be no food, and after tasting the sweet flesh of the living, he didn't want to go back to how it was before.

No, he needed them around, but not for slave labor; as food.

He pointed to an old man in another cage of humans, then a sick child in another, and each time the zombies tore them apart and fed on their corpses in the center of what had become a circle of death.

As for the remaining humans, they cowered in fear, hugging one another as they watched their oncoming fate, knowing there would be no escape.

After all, how do you escape from guards that never slept or never blinked?

Turning away from the carnage, Jonah returned to his office and studied the map. By tomorrow they would head out, more than a thousand strong, and after the next city he would have two thousand undead warriors. By the time he was through with this state there would be so many of his brethren with him there would be no stopping him.

And the humans would feel what it was like to be on the other side of the whip.

And best of all, there was nothing that could stop him.

Chapter 16

The night went slowly for the three weary survivors, the sounds of gunshots, screams, and explosions filtering into the station as well as the odor of burning buildings. Despite this they remained safe inside the police station.

But then, a few hours before dawn, they finally came under siege. It had been half past three and they were all sleeping fitfully in the main room of the station with feet propped up on chairs or desks.

A loud pounding had woken them, and it had been Brian who had investigated, hoping it was someone else who had managed to survive.

There had to be more people, how could it be that only he and the two women were the only survivors?

Pulling his Glock, he had moved to the front doors and peered through the glass. The horizon was lighter than it should be thanks to the flickering fires of the nearby buildings. A pall of smoke hung over the city like thick cumulous clouds preparing to send rain over the land.

Brian's hopes of another survivor were dashed when he saw the pounding was thanks to five ghouls who had come to investigate the police station. Their orders from Jonah were to go from building to building in a room to room search; the leader of the undead wanting to make sure every human was found.

And so the ghouls had finally reached the police station.

Brian had ducked back down and Christie had joined him, Marsha staying near the rear. She wasn't carrying a gun, not wanting one when she was offered a firearm earlier, but as the pounding continued, she was beginning to regret her decision.

"We need to go out there and take them down before they alert any others in the area," Brian said as he checked his Glock to make sure it was ready to fire. He had a full clip and there were two more on a nearby desk, but Christie shook her head in the gloom of the station.

"So what, we're just gonna go out there and start shooting? No way, we need to take them out quietly so those other ones you just spoke about don't hear us."

Brian frowned, considering her words.

"Shit, you're right, I wasn't thinking. So, you have any suggestions?"

"Yeah, actually, stay here, I'll be right back," she said and then stood and dashed across the room, weaving in between the desks.

The pounding was louder now as more ghouls joined the others. Brian went back to the window and peered outside. He saw a total of eight so far, a few other shadows moving across the street. He watched the ones walking around and saw they were spread out and weren't that fast. Like sleepy old men, they shuffled from building to building; sometimes going inside and other times just pounding on the doors.

He nodded to himself. They could take 'em, he and Christie. The trick would be to keep moving, never slow down so they could become encircled. But the other question would be how to take them down fast? He thought of the nightstick he carried on patrol, but didn't think it would do the job as quick as he needed. No, they needed something that could take down what was in essence still a human being fast, and then keep him down.

Christie reappeared and when she passed Marsha she paused. "You okay?"

Marsha nodded curtly. "I'm fine, thanks for asking. Are we gonna be okay?"

Christie flashed her a sly grin. "Yeah, I think so, but me and Brian are gonna have to go outside and deal with those deadheads or we're likely to have more out there."

"Can I help?" She asked this though she didn't really want an answer and was relieved by Christie's reply.

"No, you stay here, but come over to the door. When we go out you can close it behind us and be ready when we need to get back in, how's that?"

"Okay, fine," Marsha said, relieved she wasn't going to have to go outside.

Christie continued on to the door and Brian's eyes went wide when he saw what she was carrying.

"What the fuck are we supposed to do with those?" He asked, pointing at the two, long, eighteen inch machetes in her hands. Christie had taken them from the evidence locker; the long blades confiscated more than a month ago after some altercation between a neighbor and his overhanging tree branches has almost ended in violence.

"We're gonna use them to stop those bastards, that's what. We need to do this silently, right? And nothing is more silent than knives." She handed him one. "Here take it," she said.

Brian did and he hefted the long blade. It was almost three inches wide near the tip and then it tapered to two inches at the hilt. He had to admit, for hacking and slashing at human bodies, it would do the trick nicely.

"Come on let's not give them any more time to add to their numbers," Christie said as she moved to the door. The pounding was still continuing, flesh on wood making it sound like slabs of meat were hitting the door.

"Right behind you," Brian said as he moved next to her.

"Marsha, come here, and get ready to close the door," Christie told her, the woman doing as she was told.

Christie seemed to be in charge of the situation and Brian had no trouble deferring to her. Each of them had their strength and weaknesses, and if Christie felt confident on this endeavor, he was all for it.

"Okay, when we open the door, we hit the ones in our way and then we run down the stairs, once there we go to work," she said.

"Yeah, sounds good," Brian agreed. "I was watching some of them on the street while you were gone and they're slow. If we keep moving and hit them hard and fast, we should be okay."

"All right then, let's get this show on the road," Christie said as she moved right up to the door.

Brian followed her, and with a last look at Marsha to make sure she was ready, Christie unlocked the door, opened it, and with machete held high swung it down at the first ghoul who had been standing there with its right arm up as it prepared to pound on the door again.

But now the door was gone and a woman with a long knife was standing in front of the ghoul. Before the dead man could do anything, the blade came down and sliced off the hand at the wrist, blood pumping from the stump to splash the side of the door. But the ghouls felt no pain, and as the dead man prepared to attack, the machete thunked into its forehead, then was twisted free as the ghoul fell to the side, brains already sliding out of the large gash in its head.

Brian wasn't waiting for a chance to attack either, and he hacked at the next zombie on the stairs, his blade slashing the neck and almost severing the head from the zombie's shoulders. The head flopped back like the top of a half open can of peaches and only the remaining flesh prevented it from falling all the way off the shoulders. Brian kicked out with his boot, and the body thumped off the stairs, knocking two more ghouls off their feet like they were ten pins brought down by a strike.

Christie was still moving, dodging around the ghoul she'd taken down as she ran into the street.

"Close the door, Marsha, now!" Christie yelled and Marsha did as she was told, slamming the door as another zombie, a female, slapped rotten hands on the wood. All Marsha could do now was watch out the window, which was plated lead with reinforced wire. No simple bare hands pounding on the glass would ever break it.

Christie's eyes took in the nighttime scene in one glance. She saw two ghouls to her right with rifles in their hands, and though it still seemed so wrong to have zombies using guns, she knew she needed to take those two down before; A, they got off a shot and killed either her or Brian, or; B, they did fire which would alert any other ghouls in the area there were people in the police station.

So spinning on her heels, she powered forward, charging at the two ghouls like she was running the hundred yard dash.

The sudden appearance of Christie and Brian had left the zombies flatfooted and their dull minds had yet to figure out they were in danger, not thinking to use their guns.

That was Christie's advantage and she took it. As she ran across the street, the machete high over her head, the first ghoul with a rifle spun around to shoot her, but Christie was faster, bringing the machete down in an overhead blow that took both the zombie's arms off at the elbows. The rifle clattered to the sidewalk along with the twitching hands and she spun around to deal with the other armed ghoul. She wasn't worried about the one she'd just attacked, as without hands, it couldn't do much damage to her or Brian. The second ghoul had an extra second to raise his weapon so Christie had no choice but to take a chance. She brought her arm back with the machete and threw the blade as hard as she could at the ghoul.

The machete wasn't made for throwing and it spun in the air like a lopsided stick, but the handle struck the ghoul in the center of the face, crunching the cartilage of the dead man's face. The zombie took a step back from the blow, and by the time he was recovering, Christie had reached the dead man and bowled into him, sweeping the machete up from the ground as her left shoulder hit the ghoul's stomach head on, the rifle spinning from his dead hands to clatter on the pavement.

If the ghoul had needed to breathe, his breath would have escaped him in a gust of expelled air, but instead there was only a soft wheeze as stale air slid out of his useless lungs. Christie rolled on the sidewalk, and over the ghoul, but she was on her feet again in an instant.

Turning quickly, she raised the machete over her head yet again and brought the point of the blade down into the ghoul's chest, then she twisted it and pulled to the side, cutting a jagged line across the zombie's torso. Black and brown organs spilled out of the open cavity, and as the ghoul rolled onto its side, intestines and other miscellaneous organs spilled out to splash on the street, gleaming dully in the wan moonlight.

Christie didn't see any of this as she had already turned and was charging across the street to help Brian, who was dealing with the last three zombies. Bodies were spread out on the pavement near his feet and it was as he was fighting the last of them that he mis-stepped and tripped over a corpse, his arms pin-wheeling as he landed hard and sprawled in the middle of the street. When he fell, his machete slid from his fingers to clatter across the road and he looked up at his doom as the ghouls prepared to dive in and tear him apart.

That was when Christie charged into the fray, her blood-stained blade slashing like she was a demon from Hell. One slash took a ghoul's ear off, another lost four fingers as it reached for out for her. She slashed another in the knee, blood squirting from the wound as she danced and fought to save Brian from becoming dinner. Brian didn't waste the chance she gave him and he rolled to the side and crawled over the corpse that had tripped him, his left hand sliding almost to the elbow into the open chest cavity of the corpse. Pulling his arm free with a sucking sound, he crawled like a two-year-old until he reached his lost machete, only to hear foot-steps coming up behind him. Two things happened at the exact same time next, the first being he reached out and wrapped his palm around the handle of the machete. Then, while rolling over, he gazed up into the undead face of one of the zombies, who had followed him while Christie battled the other two. The ghoul never slowed, but seemed to actually fall on him with teeth gnashing and one hand reaching for him. The other hand was missing all four fingers and so wasn't much of a threat. So Brian did the only thing he could do in the half second before the ghoul fell on him, he raised the machete over his face and closed his eyes.

The ghoul, its weight propelling it forward, never slowed as gravity took over and its head was in a perfect line for the tip of the machete. The tip of the blade caught the ghoul in the mouth and then forced its way to the back of its head and then broke the pale skin as the head began to slide down on the machete.

Black ichor squirted out of the open mouth to splatter on Brian's face. Turning his head, he spit out what got on his lips and seeped into his mouth. He was motionless for a few seconds, the ghoul still on top of him, its remaining hand trying to pull at him, but with the head impaled on the machete, it was trapped.

With a heave of tired muscles, and a kick of his right leg, Brian pushed the ghoul off him, the machete slicing to the side and taking the top half of the ghoul's head clean off. The tongue flopped around like a fish, and the upper part of the head dropped to the ground, the eyes still flicking back and forth, now the nose touching the pavement.

The ghoul with no upper head was somehow still mobile, and it climbed to its feet and wandered into the darkness. The corpse made it no more than ten feet before the body realized there was no one in charge and it pitched forward to the asphalt, the hands still twitching in final death throes.

Brian spit out more of the foul tasting blood and when he sat up he saw the area was clear of zombies. Christie stood in the middle of a pile of corpses, her chest heaving from the exertion. Her face and chest was covered in gore and she looked like a warrior woman from one of those comic books about Conan the Barbarian that Brian had read as a kid.

"You all right?" Christie asked as she wiped her eyes clear with a clean spot of her sleeve.

"I'll live," Brian replied while getting to his feet. The top part of the severed head was next to him and the eyes looked up at him, watching his every move. Brian glanced down to see the half a head watching him, and with a snarl of disgust, he kicked it away, the head rolling on its side to land in the gutter across the street. Now the head was upside down, resembling a macabre, bloody bowl, but still the eyes flicked back and forth, the world now disjointed.

Brian walked over to Christie who appeared to be watching him with wary eyes. Then he looked over his shoulder to see she wasn't watching him, but was studying the other ghouls. There was one across the street with no arms, and it was moving away from them.

"I got it," Brian said as he turned and began moving after the escaping ghoul.

As for the zombie, it turned to see Brian and when it saw him coming after it, the legs began to move faster, as if the ghoul was trying to actually escape. This bothered Brian immensely. Was this one actually trying to escape so it could report back to whoever had sent this undead search and destroy team out in the first place?

The ghoul could only shamble, however, and in no time Brian caught up to it. He kicked it in the back of the knee and the corpse fell heavily to the asphalt. As the body hit the ground, Brian was already moving over to it, and with legs straddling both sides of the body, he brought the machete, down, once, twice, and then three times, cutting the body up and making absolutely sure the ghoul was dead.

Then, with an intake of breath after his labors, he jogged back to Christie who was waiting by the stairs.

"Should we get the guns these deadheads had?" Brian asked.

Christie shook her head. "Nah, leave 'em, we got enough, and besides, you want to strip and clean 'em so we know they're safe to use?"

He shook his head no then he added; "Hell, if I had known this shit was gonna happen I would have said we should have left here already," he said as he stepped over a body."

"Yeah, that's true, but how the hell were we supposed to know they would be searching the buildings like this?" She shook her head. "These deadheads are thinking more than they ever did before, Brian. If we don't figure out how this is happening there's no place we can run to. There's a hell of a lot more of them than us, you know."

"Yeah, I know, hell, everyone knows that," he snapped back. "But what the fuck are we supposed to do? We're two cops a year out of the academy and her," he pointed up the stairs at the doors, meaning Marsha.

"Well, that may be so, but for some reason we're still alive, and if you haven't noticed there's not that many people around like that. We can't just leave."

Brian made a face. "Fuck, yeah, we can. Look, you do whatever the hell you want, but in the morning I'm taking one of the squad cars from the motor pool like we talked about and I'm outta here." His eyes creased as he glared at her. "Are you with me or not?"

She bit her lip, her hair covered in gore, and it was an odd gesture given the circumstances. The machete in her hand dripped blood, and as she talked, she waved it around, drips of scarlet and brown flying off to land on the stairs.

"Yeah, Brian, I'm with you. It's not like I have a choice."

Brian moved past her and up the stairs, Marsha opening the door at his approach. Just as he passed her, he turned to look back down at Christie and said, "It's not like any of us have a choice, we just have to do what we can to survive, just like people did five years ago."

Christie stood in the street, the light of the nearby burning buildings lighting the sky and then she scanned the bodies in the street one last time. Brian was inside the station now and Marsha was waiting at the top of the stairs, her arms wrapped around her like she was hugging herself.

Finally, Christie turned and ascended the stone steps.

"You okay?" Marsha asked.

"Yeah, I'll be fine, especially after a shower." Then she flashed Marsha a wry grin, which looked all the more ridiculous because she was covered in blood and gore. "That is once we get that deadhead out of the shower stall."

Marsha eyes went wide. "Oh, you know about that? So why didn't you say anything?"

Marsha closed the doors after Christie entered and Christie shrugged as she padded past her. "I figured you'd say something if you wanted to, otherwise there wasn't anything to be said. I'll be in the shower." And before Marsha could reply, Christie was moving through the desks, a small amount of blood now left behind where she passed as she dripped it on the floor while she walked.

Marsha watched the policewoman go, wishing she could be as tough as Christie, then she turned, peered out the front doors one last time, her eyes taking in the corpses spread all over the street, and then she slid the bolt for the door and walked away, figuring she'd see how Brian was doing.

Chapter 17

At the break of dawn, in the rear lot of the police station, one lone squad car pulled out onto the street and headed north.

As the car drove down the street, the driver never bothered to swerve around the corpses rotting in the road. As the tires rolled over torsos, the sounds of ribcages cracking and viscous fluid squirting, filled the morning air. Inside the vehicle, the two women made disgusted faces, but Brian, behind the wheel, only grinned.

"Just making sure they're dead," he smiled as he drove over the head of an old woman, the brittle skull cracking like small fireworks were going off under the car.

His smile faltered at the stern faces of the two women and he wiped his face clear and then tried to change the subject.

"Okay, if we're lucky we can make it to the interstate and be gone before anyone knows we're out here," he said as he steered the car around a stalled truck, one of many spread out on the road.

If it wasn't for the simple fact there just wasn't a lot of people in the city anymore, he had no doubt the streets would be clogged with so many cars and trucks and there would be no way he would be able to reach the interstate before they found a spot they just couldn't navigate through. Even so, there were still more than enough vehicles scattered in the street to cause him worry, but he figured one problem at a time.

Thick black clouds of smoke still hung over the city, causing everything to take on a pale, gray color. Soot covered most of the flat surfaces and he was pretty sure a lot of the city was burning out of control.

As they drove on, they weren't alone on the streets.

Zombies by the dozens were scattered all over the place, moving in and out of buildings and stumbling through the broken windows of coffee shops and storefronts. But the ghouls were on foot, and no sooner did they realize the squad car was upon them then the car was past and heading down the road, leaving the chasing ghouls in their back trail. They all were very aware of what would happen if they did find themselves trapped on the road. If the squad car became blocked by a car accident or something similar, the three survivors would be in a mighty difficult situation.

Veering around a deserted intersection and dodging a stalled taxi cab, Brian saw the street was indeed blocked, but not by steel and metal, but by rotting flesh and bone, as more than a hundred and fifty ghouls filled the road and overflowed onto the sidewalk.

He slowed the squad car to a stop, the engine idling softly in the morning air.

"Oh my God, what do we do now?" Marsha gasped from the back seat.

"Simple, we go around 'em," Christie stated. "Right, Brian?"

"Yeah, guess so, it's not like we have any choice in the matter."

"What do you mean? Why don't we just turn around and go back the way we came?" Marsha suggested.

"Simple, I don't think they're gonna let us," Brain told her as he gestured to his rearview mirror, meaning he was looking behind the vehicle.

Marsha slowly turned in her seat and her eyes went wide with shock when she saw was what was behind them. Where there were seven score zombies in front of them, there had to be double that behind them. The ghouls weren't moving, which was odd. Since they had become violent, the undead seemed to attack any humans they came across, yet now it was like they were merely watching them. As if they had set a trap and now were waiting to see what the humans were going to do next.

"Shit, Brian," Christie said, "this doesn't look good. Where the hell did they all come from?"

Brian shook his head. "Frankly, I don't give two shits where they came from."

Then, from the undead crowd, ghouls with rifles and pistols appeared and aimed them at the squad car. Brian knew their time was up. If he stayed where they were, they would be riddled with bullets.

He lowered his head and gritted his teeth, then glanced at Marsha and Christie. "Hold on and stay down, guys, this is gonna be tricky." Then he floored the gas pedal, and for good measure hit the lights and sirens, hoping the added distraction might work in his favor.

The squad car shot forward like a rocket, barreling straight for the ghouls packed more than two dozen thick, and the women inside the car prepared themselves for the impact. Bullets ricocheted off the car, more than one finding its mark, the front windshield cracking in the right corner from a well placed shot.

The zombies never moved, holding their ground like a crowd protesting for their civil rights. They would not be moved not matter what the danger.

When the front grille and bumper of the squad car impacted the first bodies, there was a shudder of metal and the zombies exploded, yellow and brown pus as well as bloated body parts spraying across the front windshield of the vehicle, blinding Brian's view.

And perhaps that was a good thing, because as the car plowed into the undead horde, the ghouls surrounded it. One zombie was knocked over to become trapped under one of the rear tires. As it fought to free itself, it managed to tear its upper half away from its lower half, intestines trailing behind it as it turned and pounded on the lower fender of the squad car. Other ghouls were mowed down, their bodies crushed below the undercarriage. One dead woman's face bounced on the road and struck the muffler, the sizzle of burnt skin seeping up into the vehicle and making the three survivors gag.

"Get us the hell out of here!" Christie yelled as she stared at the pale faces battering the glass on all sides.

"I'm trying!" Brian screeched, slamming the transmission into drive and trying to free themselves. But the instant the squad car had surged forward, the zombies behind them had also moved forward and now they were surrounding the car on all sides. Hundreds of hands slapped against the metal body of the squad car, the vehicle shaking back and forth on its shocks like it was a small boat caught in rough waters. The roof began to bend from the weight of the onslaught and Marsha screamed when the window to her left shattered, spraying safety glass on her.

Neither Brian nor Christie spoke, realizing their dire predicament. Christie reached onto the floor by her feet and picked up a .45 salvaged from the police armory, while Brian unsheathed his Glock, squeezing the grip so tight his knuckles turned white. Both of them were terrified and it was only their training as police officers that had them keeping a level head.

And then Christie's window imploded, spraying glass cubes across her legs and face. She turned away, not wanting to get glass in her eyes and then swung around and shoved the barrel of her .45 into the mouth of the first ghoul that tried to reach in and grab her. Teeth broke and the tempered metal slid into the gaping maw of a mouth and she fired, blowing half the zombie's head clean off. But the ghoul was still active and dead hands reached inside, trying to wrap around her arms. Cursing a blue streak, she maneuvered the muzzle of the gun higher and fired again, this time the lead slug blowing out a large chunk of the ghoul's brain. The body slumped over the door sill, but was quickly dragged out by its undead brethren as another tried to reach in. The only saving grace was that only one ghoul could come at her at a time thanks to the small window opening. She fired again, sending a steel jacketed slug through the zombie's eye, a larger chunk of the back of its head splattering the pale faces behind it. Then that one was yanked clear and another dove in. Christie fired again and again, but knew her supply of ammunition was limited, so she clamped her jaw tight and continued to fight, knowing the second she stopped she was dead.

Brian's window imploded next, cascading glass shards spraying his face and catching in his hair. Spitting glass cubes, he swung his Glock in the face of the first ghoul, a little old lady who had been trained as a maid. He shot her in the nose, clearing her sinuses forever, and the head snapped back and away from him. But no sooner did she fall away then another ghoul took her place, teeth gnashing at him. He fired again, the round hitting the ghoul point blank in the eye, the orb seeming to disintegrate as the bullet left the barrel of the Glock and plowed through its head like a warm knife through butter. Barely seeing the ghoul fall away, he shifted his aim and targeted the next face, shooting again and again as the Glock heated up in his hand.

Marsha was unarmed, and as she fought off hands reaching for her, the other window exploded inward, shards of glass landing on the seat like hail. One ghoul managed to get the door open, and as Marsha screamed for help, she was pulled kicking and screaming from the squad car. Brian saw her being taken, but there was nothing he could do. The front windshield was nothing but rotten faces, blood and pus now covering the glass like a coat of ice. He glanced in the rearview mirror to see the back window was the same; body upon body flowing over the car like running water.

There would be no escape, he knew, and he glanced at Christie as she fired another shot into a decayed face. Then, as she shifted her aim and squeezed the trigger, her gun clicked dry and there would be no time to reload. The gun was yanked from her hand by a gray limb and she was grabbed with grips of iron, the ghouls now trying to pull her out of her seat.

She screamed and kicked as she tried to hold on to the dashboard and Brian could do nothing for her. The second he stopped to help her, the bodies on his side would reach in and he would suffer the same fate as her.

Then Christie was being pulled out of the squad car as she shrieked in terror, and as he watched her boots slide through the shattered window, he let out his own scream of loss.

Then a dead hand slapped his face and a finger slid into his mouth. He bit down instinctively and cold, congealed blood slid into his mouth, the taste reminding him of the time he'd bitten into a rotten, hard-boiled egg by accident, after leaving it in his fridge for too long. Spitting out the fetid digit, he gagged as the foul taste managed to crawl down his throat. Resisting the urge to vomit, he fired again at another pale face. The inside of the squad car was painted in black and yellow ichor, a few splotches of red thrown in for good measure. Bodily fluids dripped down from the headliner like pudding, and he knew there would be no way he was going to escape this trap alive.

He could hear Marsha and Christie screaming over the undead moans and knew they must be getting torn apart, so knowing all was lost, he realized there was only one way out.

So after shooting one more ghoul in the face, knowing he was down to his last few rounds, he pulled the Glock back, stared at the steaming barrel covered in flesh for a faction of a second, and then jammed it into his own mouth, the top knub on the muzzle scraping tender skin in the upper half of his mouth.

He had time for one brief prayer, hoping he would be going to Heaven and not Hell, and then he squeezed the trigger, the bullet shooting straight up and into his brain, pulping it to putty as it exited out the top of his skull.

Brain matter and bone fragments splattered the headliner and his skull snapped back, bounced off the headrest and then slumped forward, but by then he knew no pain.

Dead hands reached inside the car and wrapped around his still form as a geyser of blood shot out of his head wound. His glazed eyes saw nothing as he was pulled from the squad car and ripped apart by two dozen hands, his head going off in one direction while his limbs went off in others. His torso was ripped open and dried, flaking hands reached in and tore at his insides, the warm organs quickly feasted on by fifty mouths, each tearing into the squishy entrails with gusto.

Soon there was nothing left of Brian but one gore-filled boot, his belt, and a few bloody and tattered pieces of his pants as the ghouls feasted on his flesh like it was the last supper of Christ.

Chapter 18

Marsha's world was upside down as she was dragged out of the squad car like a hog going to the slaughter house. She screamed as loud as she could and tried to fight back while waiting to feel the pain of teeth sinking into her body.

But it didn't come.

All her limbs were held in place, the fingers squeezing into her flesh like small spears, but she wasn't harmed. Though fingers tangled in her hair, they did not pull enough to hurt her, but she was in too much terror to notice just yet. Pale dead faces stared at her, moaning and wailing flooding her ears and blocking out all sound.

But then she took a moment to realize no one was eating her.

She could hear the gunshots of Christie and Brian as they tried to fend off the zombies, but she was already ten feet away from the car and still moving.

Like she was a beach ball floating over the heads of the crowd at a concert, she was carried away from the car. Below her, on the street, were the bodies of ghouls who had been trampled by their brethren. The standing ghouls paid them no mind, and simply stepped over or on them, flattening the flesh and organs to a red, gruel-like mush. She spotted a severed head, the flesh peeled off the skull, on the road as it was kicked about, and she was shocked to see the eyes look up at her, the mouth curve up in a rictus of a grin. Then a zombie's foot kicked the head and it was lost amongst the dozens of legs.

As she was carried, the redolence of death and decay was overwhelming. She had never realized how truly bad the zombies smelled. Usually there would only be one or two at a time together she remembered, and even then they were usually sprayed with perfumes so they wouldn't smell so bad. But now, these wild zombies, as she had come to think of them, had no such covering and the true odor of rot suffused her olfactory canals, making her want to gag. Flies were everywhere, buzzing over the mob like massive thunder clouds and crows and seagulls dove in and out as they tried to tear off pieces of the ghoul's flesh which hung in tatters like torn clothing.

In what seemed like forever, but was in fact only minutes, she finally found herself coming to the end of the crowd.

She was never attacked, which was odd, and though she wasn't complaining, she didn't understand why she was still alive.

Struggling to free herself, while the undead faces close by watched her, she twisted and writhed in their grasp, but eventually realized there was no escape. All around her the ghouls milled about, as if they were waiting for something. Then she saw movement to her left and soon the crowd opened and she saw Christie, who was also being carried. The policewoman was kicking and fighting, and as she was brought near to Marsha, the policewoman kicked out with her left boot and managed to flatten a nose. But if the ghoul cared that it now had no sniffer, it gave no inclination.

With yellow pus dripping out of its shattered nose, it forced her to within a few feet of Marsha.

"Marsha? You're still alive?" Christie gasped as she struggled to free herself in vain.

"I could say the same thing about you," Marsha replied as she stood still amidst the ghouls.

"But why haven't they killed us?" Christie asked.

"Don't know, but are you complaining about it?"

Christie's mouth opened and closed as if she hadn't thought about it before.

One last gunshot filled the air over the moans of the dead and both women looked up in the direction of the squad car.

"Brian?" Marsha asked.

Christie shook her head. "I don't know. He was in the car and then I got pulled out. I don't know what happened to him."

They received their answer a few minutes later when a ghoul stumbled by with a severed arm in its hand. Still gripped in the dead palm of the severed arm was Brian's Glock. Christie knew instantly the man was gone and she uttered a sob, but then stopped herself. Though she had liked Brian and felt terrible he was dead, at the moment she was more worried about her own survival.

"What are they going to do to us?" Marsha asked as she watched a ghoul walk by her, vigorously chewing on the arm like it was a chicken leg, scarlet tendons and gristle stretching from its mouth while it fed.

"I don't know, but it can't be good," she hissed as she tried to pull her arm free of the zombie holding it. All she received for her trouble was a punch to the face, a ghoul slamming its fist into her cheek so hard her head rocked to the side.

Spitting blood, Christie glared at the ghoul.

"Try that again, you fuckin' deadhead when I've got my hands free," she snarled.

The ghoul didn't reply, but turned and waved his arm as if he was instructing the others to move out. Neither Christie nor Marsha knew anything about the zombies. Neither knew how they had become more intelligent, some thinking and reasoning. One of these ghouls was the one who waved the others onward, and as a tide ebbs and flows on the shore, slowly, the zombies began turning and leaving the street.

It took more than twenty minutes for all the ghouls to depart the street, and when they were finally gone, the last zombie turning the corner, all that was left was the battered, gore-covered squad car and the bloody footprints on the pavement, plus more than two dozen ghouls who had been taken down by Christie and Brian before they had been overwhelmed

A few ghouls were still moving on the asphalt, and though they would never catch up to the receding undead crowd, they began crawling onward; legs dragging behind them like cordwood, as they, too, headed off in the direction of the marching undead mob.

Soon the street was empty of all but the truly dead. It wasn't long before seagulls and crows appeared, each fighting for a piece of the fetid meat now lying in the sun. One crow snagged a juicy tidbit and took flight, only to be hounded by three seagulls who wanted the tender morsel for themselves. The crow dodged and weaved in the air, but the seagulls were able to block its every move. Finally, the crow lost its hold on the gobbet of flesh and the meat tumbled to the ground below, only to be plucked out of the sky by one of the seagulls.

The birds would feed well today, but then, since the plague had come down and consumed mankind five years ago, the birds had always fed well.

Chapter 19

More than an hour later, after Christie and Marsha were carried like satchels of meat on the shoulders of the ghouls, they arrived at the waterfront.

The sun was high in the sky and the ocean breeze wasn't nearly strong enough to wash the stink of death and decay from so many rotting bodies gathered together in one place.

The two women were brought to a warehouse on the edge of the docks, and then ushered inside with the horde of undead men and women while more than two hundred zombies remained outside to wander around like sleep walking guards.

Inside the warehouse, Marsha and Christie's senses were immediately blasted with the odor of feces and blood, mixed in with rotting meat. The miasma of sickness seemed to hang in the air like pea soup and Marsha ended up throwing up all over the nearest ghoul. If the ghoul was bothered by the green bile now covering its shirt and pants, it showed no outward inclination.

"Oh my God, want the fuck is all this?" Christie gasped as she was led with Marsha to one of the steel cages filled with living humans.

As the ghouls approached the makeshift gate to the cage, the humans shrank back, assuming they were about to lose one of their number again. Christie tried to see everything at once, her police training keeping her strong. She saw over to the left a large area where the floor was covered an inch thick in blood and gore. Here, a few ghouls were still feeding on the last slaughtered human. Off to her right was a large metal staircase that led up to a door with a plate-glass window on the side of it. She saw a shadow moving in the room at the window, but she couldn't make out who it might be. Then she was shoved into the cage and any further observation would have to wait. She fell to the floor, whacking her knee, and no sooner did she land then Marsha fell on top of her. Both women fell in a heap and the ghouls receded, closing the gate and moving away, their shoulders hunched over like cavemen.

Thirty ghouls remained behind to guard the humans while the others wandered away mindlessly. Their task now finished, they went back to just being zombies, with no particular aspiration. A few shuffled over to the gore-covered circle and began scraping up bloody gruel from the floor, slurping the mush into their mouths as they tried to gather what sustenance they could from the fetid porridge. Others seemed to just wander away, like brain-dead hippies after a particularly heavy acid trip.

Christie and Marsha were helped to their feet by a few of the closer humans. Then the crowd parted and a white-haired man, sixty or so, in filthy clothes stepped up to them, holding his hand out in greeting.

"Hello, my name's Thomas and I guess you could say I'm the spokesman for this little group."

"Spokesman for what?" Christie asked, her eyes staring at the haggard and drawn faces around her. Most were middle age, a few in their twenties. A dozen or so were children, and the little ones hugged the legs of those who were watching over them, their eyes wide with tears and fear. "Who the hell are you people and what am I doing here?"

"Yeah, that goes for me too," Marsha added.

The man shrugged. "I wish I had more to tell you, but I don't. A day ago most of us were pulled out of our beds and dragged from our homes by the deadheads who used to be our workers. Are you aware they seem to have become sentient?"

"I'm a cop, of course I know," Christie snapped.

"Oh," the man said. "My apologies. You're not in uniform, so I just assumed..."

"Forget it, it doesn't matter anyway," Christie said. Both she and Brian had changed before they had left the station, deciding their uniforms were redundant.

'Though I still don't understand how this is happening," Christie told him. "How can they act like this? Who's telling them what to do?"

"There's a deadhead up in that office, that's who," a haggard-faced woman said from behind Christie, her dirty hand pointing to the plate-glass window.

Christie followed the finger and studied the window again. There was a shadowy form there, yes, but if it was a deadhead it was anyone's guess.

"That's ridiculous. You're saying one of them is in charge? But how?"

The old man shrugged again. "No one knows and frankly it doesn't matter how. The fact is, it's happening and if we don't get out of here we're all doomed."

"Why?" Marsha asked.

The old man frowned, lowering his voice so as to not upset the others in the cage. "Because the only reason they're keeping us here is for food. They're eating us now, Miss, and sooner or later they're gonna eat us all."

Marsha and Christie didn't reply, knowing the man was correct. It made sense. For some reason the ghouls had been trained to not kill the people they found in the city. They had been instructed to bring them back to the warehouse where they were now kenneled like cattle waiting for slaughter.

"So what happens now?" Christie asked.

The old man shook his head in defeat. "Now, young lady, we wait to die, unless a miracle arrives to save us."

"What? You can't wait to be saved. We need to do it ourselves," Christie told him forcefully.

"Uh-huh, and how do you suggest this we do this? We're surrounded by more than a thousand deadheads and to top it off we're in a cage." He sighed heavily. "No, my dear, I'm afraid all we can do is make peace with God and wait till the end comes."

"He's right, we're all dead," another woman said from behind her, a few others agreeing.

Christie eyed each face close to her, her mouth curled up into a sneer.

"Well, you people might be giving up, but I'm not. As long as I can breathe I can fight and dammit, so can you. There's got to be a way out of here, we just need to find it."

The old man stepped aside, his head low. "I wish what you said was truthful, but as you will find out soon enough, you're as doomed as the rest of us. Now, if you'll excuse me, I want to be with my wife for however long we have left on this earth." He smiled then, which seemed odd given the present circumstances. "You know, I thought it was a miracle that allowed us both to be spared from the plague all those years ago. Now it looks like the ones who died back then were the lucky ones. At least they went quick." Then he was gone, lost in the bodies of the crowd.

"What are we gonna do?" Marsha asked Christie as she watched the deadpan faces of the other humans staring at them.

"We fight, that's what. I don't know how, but we do. We have to do it, if not for ourselves then for Brian."

Marsha nodded, agreeing with her. "Do you...do you think he suffered much?" Marsha asked about Brian.

Christie turned to her, placing both hands on Marsha's shoulders.

"Did he suffer? I don't know, but if they tore him apart, then yeah, I bet he suffered a lot. But that doesn't matter because he's dead and we're still alive. And we're gonna stay that way. You with me?"

"Yeah, I'm with you," Marsha said as she held back a sob. She was scared, even more scared than all the other times combined. She thought it was the waiting that got to her the most, waiting for what was going to happen. She was reminded of a documentary she had seen many years ago.

It was set during WW2 at a concentration camp. The prisoners had been lined up on the ground in neat rows and a German officer was walking up to each prisoner and shooting each man or woman in the head. Pop, then the head would snap forward into the dirt, then another pop, followed by dozens more. She had imagined what it would have been like to be one of the last prisoners in line, to know what was coming, but still have to wait almost patiently for that German officer to reach you, then place the gun behind your head and squeeze the trigger. But what if when he squeezed the trigger, while you lay there, weeping into the dirt, the gun was empty? So the officer calmly reloaded his gun, shaking out spent shells and then adding new ones, all the while you waited for him to finish, knowing it would be your death. That you would cease to exist, though the world would continue on without you.

That was the worst thing about dying, she supposed, to know that though to her the world truly consisted of the universe of one, of herself, and all else gravitated around her, in the end, if she died, the world would continue.

The sun would rise and set, the moon would float across the sky each night. And people would live and then die. The world was autonomous to her, and though each human being liked to think that wasn't so, in reality every person was inconsequential.

Just another ant on the massive anthill called the Earth.

So like that German prisoner who waited for the gun to be reloaded, so too, did she feel that pain in her gut as she waited for whatever was going to happen next.

And she had a sinking feeling she wasn't going to like it.

Chapter 20

Marsha and Christie saw just how bad things could get a little more than an hour later. All the prisoners were huddled together in one corner of the cage, the same thing happening in the other cages across the warehouse.

All faces turned to glance up at the balcony where the offices were, the plate-glass window dark, the lights off inside. They knew if that door opened it would spell the death for one of them.

But then the door did open, and with a gasp of fear from the humans below, a zombie strode out. Where the other ghouls were uncoordinated, this ghoul seemed strong and in control of its body.

The ghoul pointed to the cage Marsha was in and then at one of the other cages near the south wall. Immediately the zombies on the warehouse floor went to the cages, unlocking the gates and opening them, pulling out a hostage from each cage. If the prisoner had any thought of escape, it was quickly squashed when they saw the hundreds of ghouls waiting for them outside the cage.

One was a man in his late seventies, the other, a woman, stunning in her beauty.

The man and woman were dragged to the gore-filled circle and then released. They stood together, petrified, holding one another, and though they knew not the other, now they were intimately entangled in their fear of what was to come.

Both had seen what had happened to the other hostages thrown into the circle of blood and knew what was coming next.

The woman cried, her shoulders shuddering as she tried to get as close to the old man as possible. As for the man, though he tried to stay defiant, his chin twitched and tears rolled down his cheeks to splash in the blood at his feet.

In truth, he wasn't so sad for his own demise. He was almost eighty and had lived a full life, but since his wife had died in the plague, his life had been without meaning. On many ways he welcomed death, though this was hardly the way he would have preferred to go out. But the woman in his arms was young and full of life, and it saddened him deeply that she was going to die at such a young age, and so horribly. It was only more bittersweet that the woman had managed to survive the plague only to become food for the undead monsters before them.

The zombie in the shape of a man on the balcony raised his hand in the air, the thumb facing upward. A slight murmur went through the undead crowd and both Marsha and Christie watched with amazement as the ghouls remained rooted to their spots, none attacking the shivering couple.

But then the ghoul turned his fist so his thumb was pointing downward, and no sooner was the gesture completed, than the ghouls swarmed into the circle, reaching and grabbing for the man and woman.

The old man did his best to try and protect the woman, but he was attacked from all sides and he was old; he didn't last long. In seconds, he was on the floor, his back now splattered with gore as his clothes were ripped from his wrinkled frame.

Next to him, the woman screamed as the same was done to her, and no sooner were her clothes removed then she felt the cold bite of nails and teeth on her warm flesh.

The man screamed then, the screams soon turning to shrieks of agony as he was slowly ripped apart one bloody piece at a time. His arms were severed from his torso, followed by his legs, and in less than a minute he was nothing but a bloody torso with a head attached. His eyes budged from their sockets in agony, but he didn't see anymore, the pain was so great, but still he cursed the undead horde as they devoured him while he watched.

He opened his mouth to scream yet again but it was muffled when an ocher-colored hand was shoved into his mouth, grabbing his tongue like a slippery eel and yanking it out, the blood spurting like a small water fountain. By now the old man was losing consciousness from blood loss, and as he howled his pain, his head was twisted off like a cork screw; finally tendons and muscle snapping as the head was severed from his shoulders. It was quickly pulled away where a promiscuous ghoul then shoved a hand into the open neck cavity to secure the vermillion tendrils within.

As for the woman, she fared no better. Her body was glorious, tight abs and silky skin, and like veal to a meat lover, the ghouls dove in and began tearing her apart. Her breasts were sliced with nails sharpened by death, as the flesh had receded, and hunks of the fatty tissue once called her breasts found mouths. The woman's hair was covered in blood and gore, and it shined in the dim light of the warehouse as the zombies tore into her once stunning body, pulling kidney, spleen, and intestines out to spill out on the floor so that the others nearby could gorge themselves on the warm innards.

The woman didn't last as long as the man, as before she suffered too much, a bloody hand reached in and ripped her thumping heart from her chest, feeding on the still pulsing organ. The woman died in silence, her last scream still on her soft lips, that is until a ghoul leaned over, and as if the dead man was making love to the woman, he bit down and ripped the lips off with his brown teeth, chewing happily. As for the woman, without lips she now showed the world her death smile, her teeth and gums glistening in the wan light, that is until yet another ghoul dove in and began tearing the flesh from her skull, much like a famished diner peeling the cooked chicken skin from a newly roasted bird.

Marsha and Christie, as well as the other hostages watched in silence, some crying, the children pushed to the back of the crowd so they wouldn't see what would eventually be their fate.

The feeding went on for another ten minutes until most of the ghouls had their fill. But there were more than eight hundred ghouls in the warehouse, the other two hundred outside, and they needed much more than two humans to feed them all.

So the zombie on the balcony put his hands together and spread them wide, as if he was parting water. All the ghouls that had fed, now covered in glistening bright red, moved to the sides and the ones that had not touched the human meat now moved into the circle.

It was their turn to feed.

The zombie on the balcony then pointed to the cages again and the ghouls went back for more food.

This time Marsha was picked and she was dragged screaming out into the warehouse while another man was taken from another nearby cage.

Both were put in the circle, and as Marsha cried tears of loss for her own demise, the man tried to console her.

The zombie on the balcony raised his hand again, his thumb up and both Marsha and the man knew what was going to happen next.

And then the thumb went down and the ghouls swarmed in. But this man was more powerful than the old man from before and he fought and punched and kicked to keep the ghouls away from them. But of course there were far too many to fight for long, and in less than ten seconds, he was overwhelmed and brought down, teeth and nails sinking into his flesh as he screamed for them to stop.

Marsha was next, but as the ghouls surrounded her and prepared to bring her to the floor, a loud scream from above, guttural in its animosity, stopped the ghouls in their tracks. Only the zombies hovering over the dead man continued feeding, as they were lost in their hunger, but the others trained to obey their leader without question stopped.

Marsha didn't move, her chest heaving as dead hands held her once again. She didn't know what had happened, but she wasn't complaining, and her eyes tried to seek out Christie in the cage beyond. But there were far too many bodies in her line of sight to see the policewoman.

The zombie from the balcony now walked down the steel stairs and then crossed the warehouse floor. When he reached the crowd of undead, they parted for him, their master flowing through them like a magnet, repelling its polar opposite.

A low moan came from the ghouls sounding a little like prayer or chanting.

The zombie walked through the crowd until he was at the edge of the circle and he waved for the zombies holding Marsha to bring her to him.

Marsha fought them a little, but she was no match, and soon she was standing in front of the zombie.

As she stared into the milky white eyes she saw nothing familiar, but then her eyes glided over the pale, rotting face to see the white streak of hair in his dark mane and her mouth fell open in absolute shock.

"Seth? Is that you? But how? It can't be, you're dead," she gasped as she stared at the zombie. How can this be, her fiancé was dead, she knew this for a fact. She had seen his body in the hospital after he'd died. She had held his cold hand before they had wheeled him away forever.

The zombie called Jonah, formerly Seth, nodded and then pointed to his throat. He tried to speak and only a growl issued.

"You can't talk? Oh, okay, but this is impossible, it can't be you," she said.

Jonah reached out his right hand and brought it to Marsha's temple. His index finger extended, and he carefully brushed the errant blonde hair off her forehead.

Marsha sucked in a breath of disbelief.

Seth used to do that very same thing. She remembered countless times as they would be together, at the movies or walking in the park, her long bangs would cover her forehead, just touching her eyebrows, and he would reach out and brush them away. It had become a ritual with them later, and as he did this now, she knew the zombie in front of her was her lost love.

"But I don't understand. If it's really you, why are you doing this? You were a good person, Seth, why are you killing all these innocent people?"

Jonah shook his head, closing his eyes as his former humanity raged inside him. But in the end it was who he was now, a ghoul, that won the battle.

Deciding there was nothing to be said as he could never explain to her what he was doing; he grabbed the closest zombie with some intelligence and pointed to the cage, then to Marsha.

The zombie understood and in seconds Marsha was being ushered back to her cage.

"Wait, Seth, what's happening? Don't let them put me back. I want to talk to you. You don't have to do this, Seth, we can make things right!"

Seth turned away from her, either not listening or not wanting to hear her, and then he walked back to the balcony. When he was overlooking his people once again, he pointed to one of the other cages and pointed his fist down, thumb facing the floor.

The gesture was understood. Though Marsha was off the menu, another human would suffice.

As Marsha was tossed back into the cage, another human, a boy of ten, was pulled from another cage. The child cried tears of horror as he was dumped into the circle of blood and gore. As the boy screamed for his mother, the ghouls swarmed in, and though small, the boy was tender and served as an excellent repast.

Marsha was sick with guilt, knowing she was spared and the child killed instead. The other prisoners now moved away from her, as if she was tainted by some foul evil. All had seen her exchange with Jonah and knew whatever had happened wasn't right.

Christie didn't feel that way and she moved next to Marsha who was huddled on the ground, staring at the floor in disbelief at what had happened.

"What the fuck was that all about? Why didn't they eat you?"

Marsha shook her head, her blonde tresses falling over her face.

"I...I don't know really, but that deadhead...I know this is hard to believe, but that's my fiancé, Seth. He died from the plague five years ago."

"No, shit? You're being serious?" Christie asked as she turned and looked to the balcony. The zombie was there again, like a king watching over his kingdom.

"So he spared you for some reason, huh?"

Marsha nodded. "I think he remembers who he is. He...he did something that Seth used to do when we were together. There's no way it can't be him, and his hair. That white streak in it. Seth had that too, it was a birth mark. I never saw anyone else with it for as long as I'd known him. It's got to be him."

Christie plopped down on the floor as the other prisoners stared at them, murmuring softly together.

"Oh, fuck off, all of you. What just happened might be our ticket outta here," Christie snapped, the prisoners then turning away, not used to the ferocity of Christie. A few had been brave after first arriving, but they had quickly realized their fate and had lost hope. All the prisoners knew Christie would soon feel that way, also. It didn't take very long for the realization of just how doomed they all were to sink in. Maybe after a few more feedings.

"Look, Marsha, I think there might be a way to get us out of here, but I don't really know just yet. I need a little longer to work it all out. I got the idea when that deadhead stopped the killing and saved you."

Marsha looked up into the policewoman's eyes.

"What are you taking about?"

"A way to save us all," Christie said. "If that deadhead thinks you and he are supposed to be married, and he spared you once, that means he might come back here for you again."

"Yeah, so?"

"So, I don't know. I told you, I haven't figured that part out yet, but I will. Now you rest up while I go talk to some of the others."

Marsha nodded slightly, still in a daze.

How could this be happening? Maybe none of this was true and she would wake up any second in her bed at home, her aunt coming to see how she was, and she would realize it had all been a bad dream.

As she let her head sink between her legs, she closed her eyes and prayed that was so, though when she saw the bloody gruel covering her sneakers from being in the death circle, and remembered the screams of the ten-year-old boy, she knew it wasn't so.

If she was dreaming, then she was in the worst nightmare of her life, and she didn't think she'd be waking up anytime soon.

Chapter 21

The smell was atrocious inside the warehouse.

Between the rotting bodies of almost a thousand ghouls, the circle of death filled with blood and gore, and the feces and urine pile where each cage of humans had chosen to use as a bathroom, it was all Marsha could do to stop herself from gagging every few seconds.

The ghouls could have cared less about such things. The warehouse smelled like the worst outhouse in history, multiplied by a hundred, no, a thousand times.

Flies were everywhere, feeding on whatever they could find. Maggots had already begun growing in the offal, the small white larva squirming about as new life filled them.

Marsha almost envied the disgusting little worms. At least they were free.

Two hours had passed since Marsha had been saved from being torn apart and she sat against the wall of the cage, sulking. All around her the other prisoners moved about. Some were crying, but others had seemed to accept their fate, that death was inevitable and there would be no escaping it. As they moved back and forth in the cage, resembling the zombies that guarded them, Marsha thought they looked like terminal cancer patients who had come to accept their ailment.

It was the children that broke her heart the most. They clung to whatever adult was watching them at the moment, some crying for their lost mother or father. They were so young and now they had no future.

Thinking like that made her so angry she wanted to scream, images of the ten-year-old boy being ripped apart flooding back into her head. She tried to close her eyes but the images only grew stronger. Eventually she stood up, opened her eyes, and tried to walk around like the others were, hoping the movement would distract her from what would happen next.

After the boy had been killed, three more prisoners had been taken from the cages and fed to the ghouls, then it seemed Seth had gone into the office and left them alone. The other ghouls merely strolled around in circles, like sleepwalkers, or sat on the floor and stared into the nothingness that was their world.

It was eerie watching them. These humanoid creatures that had been their gardeners, waiters and trash collectors, had somehow turned the tables on their owners and were now in charge.

She wondered what the rest of the country was doing about what had happened in the city. Surely they must know what was going on by now. She had to wonder why no one had come to save them yet. Why hadn't the army come charging in like in the movies and destroyed all the ghouls, saving the frightened humans.

She looked up to see Christie over by the north edge of the cage. She kept watching the zombies as they moved past her. There was a hole in the fence around waist height and Christie's left hand was jutting through the opening, her fingers squeezing over and over again.

Marsha began watching her and realized Christie was waiting for one particular ghoul to move closer. Deciding she was curious, Marsha walked over to her.

"Whatcha doin'?"

"See that old deadhead over there? The one with the beehive bun?" Christie said as she gestured with her chin to an old woman, the ghoul wearing the guise of a maid.

"What about her?"

"She's got something I want, but she won't come over here. I even tried calling to her but she's a damn deadhead, she's stupid."

Marsha said nothing, only watching.

The two stayed in that position for another twenty minutes and Marsha was opening her mouth to tell Christie she was going to go sit down again when a crowd of zombies moved like a wave towards the dead maid. Though stupid, all the zombies had basic instincts, and as the crowd moved toward her, the old woman began shuffling out of the way. This new movement caused her to begin to migrate towards Christie's spot, and just when Marsha thought the old ghoul was going to swerve out of the way, she was close enough for Christie to reach out and snag something from out of her waist.

"Hah, got it, I knew if I was patient it would pay off," she said victoriously as she pulled her hand back through the hole and showed Marsha her prize.

Marsha stared at the thin knitting needle, the tip covered in brown ichor from where it had been jabbed into the old ghoul's side. Evidently, the zombie had been attacked at some point, perhaps by someone trying to defend themselves, and the knitting needle had become embedded in the thin frame of the old maid.

But now Christie had it, and she held it up like she was holding the Holy Grail.

"It's a knitting needle, big deal," Marsha said blandly.

Her stomach was growling and she was miserable. Then she felt guilty for being hungry. The other prisoners had been in the warehouse far longer than her and they were on the point of wanting to eat their shoes. With more than a day having passed with none of them getting any food or water, the next few days ahead would be worse. Some were already wishing for death as they began to waste away from the inside out.

Christie lowered her arm and moved closer to Marsha. She did this without thinking as none of the humans cared what she was saying, and the closest ghouls were too stupid to understand the conversation.

"No, silly, you don't get it, I know it's just a knitting needle, but if it was used like an ice pick it could take out a deadhead." She made a motion to her left ear with the needle, like she was jamming into her ear canal and into her brain. She finished by twisting the needle, though the tip never entered her ear, of course.

Marsha stared at her blandly, not understanding where the policewoman was going with her line of discussion. She didn't mean to be obtuse, but she was still in a state of shock from everything that had happened.

Christie sighed and decided to just spell it out.

"Look, that deadhead that saved you used to be your fiancé, right?"

Marsha nodded.

"Right, and if he saved you once it's possible he might come and get you again. You follow me?"

Marsha nodded slightly.

"Okay, well if you didn't notice, he seems to be in charge of the others. Who's to say what would happen if he was taken out. The other deadheads might just become lost with no leader." Then she frowned as she thought of something else. "Or then again they might all just go nuts and kill us all. Either way, we're all dead so there's really not that much to lose, you agree?"

Marsha took a step back.

"What a second, you want me to kill Seth? How can you ask me to do that? I love him," she gasped. A few other prisoners were now listening to the conversation, all very interested. If there was a chance they could escape, no matter how slim, they wanted in.

"He's not Seth, he's a deadhead, Marsha, get that through your fuckin' head," Christie snapped as she stepped so close to Marsha the woman could smell the cop's bad breath. "He's a zombie now; whoever he was is gone. You know that, you just don't want to admit it."

Marsha closed her eyes and began shaking her head in denial, not wanting to here what the woman was saying.

"No, I won't do it, and you can't make me. I thought I'd lost him and now I've found him again. It's him, and you'll see. I'll get him to release everyone, I just need some time."

"What kind of shit are you spoutin' lady," a tall man in a filthy t-shirt said as he interjected himself into the conversation. "If you think by killin' that dead asshole on the balcony might get us all free then by God Himself you need to do it, and pronto."

Marsha turned to the man, staring at his dirty face as she wondered who he was and why he felt he had an opinion.

"Fuck off, and leave me alone!" Marsha screamed at him, the man stepping back from her fury. "Nobody is going to tell me what I can and can't do, you hear me!"

The man was about to speak when the older man they had first met stopped the tall man, pulling him away from Marsha. The two men began arguing about the merits of what Christie was saying, but Marsha heard none of it.

Christie moved closer again, her hands held out to console her, only her left hand still held the knitting needle.

"Marsha, wait, you have to listen," she pleaded.

"No! I don't have to listen to anything you say, now leave me alone!" She turned and moved away, pushing through the throng of prisoners until she was at the far end of the cage. She stopped at the fence and had to take a step back when a zombie moved at her from the opposite side of the metal grating. The face of the ghoul was sunken, the eyes set deep in a protruding forehead. Yellow and green snot ran out of the nose, and when the ghoul opened its mouth, maggots could be seen within, a thick coating of blood staining the teeth scarlet. As the mouth opened, a miasma of death wafted out and Marsha gagged as she inhaled the foul odor. Then she moved away and found a place bereft of humans or ghouls. Sitting on her butt, she brought her knees up to her chest and laid her head on her knees, rocking back and forth like a child.

Christie was insane. To kill Seth when she had just found him again? She could never do that. She loved him and even after five years that love was as strong as the day he had left her.

Her emotions were a mess and she closed her eyes, tears sliding down her cheeks. Deep down inside herself she knew what Christie had said made sense, but she didn't want to admit it to herself.

Full of conflict and self-doubt, she began to cry, while all around her the trapped humans and the zombies outside the cage moved about, one waiting to die, and the other waiting to live, only at the moment either one was interchangeable.

Chapter 22

Fifteen minutes after Marsha had sat down to think about everything Christie had said, the door to the office with the plate-glass window opened and the zombie called Jonah stepped out onto the balcony, only this time he had three more zombies with him.

These three had managed to hold onto a rudimentary intelligence and they now descended the stairs, following the orders Jonah had given them. Each carried a purloined M-16, taken from dead soldiers the day before.

The ghouls crossed the warehouse floor until they had reached the cage with Marsha in it. Opening it up, one pointed to her with the barrel of his rifle, and as the other prisoners moved aside, one of the ghouls went and picked up Marsha off the floor.

She didn't fight them, knowing they weren't bringing her to the circle of death, and with a brief glance to some of the faces watching her like she was a traitor, she let the zombies lead her out of the cage.

Just before she exited the cage, Christie ran up to her and thrust the knitting needle into her right hand, her body hiding the action from the eyes of the ghouls.

"Take this and do what has to be done, for all our sakes," she begged, and then was shoved away by one of the ghouls.

Marsha took the knitting needle, not knowing why she did it, but as she was pushed out of the cage, she slid the needle under her shirt, hiding it from view. While she walked, the tip pinched her flesh; a constant reminder to what Christie wanted her to do, though she was wont to do it.

As she crossed the warehouse, she was able to see inside the other cages better. If she had expected something other than what had been in her cage, she was disappointed. The same haggard and hopeless faces gazed back at her as she passed them, a few calling out to her and wishing her luck. These human hadn't seen everything that had happened and just assumed she was like them.

While Marsha was led away, Christie was gathering the people in the cage with her, trying to tell them what Marsha was going to do, and when it happened they all needed to take the chance and attack the ghouls. Some protested but most still had a small spark of fight left in them and more than half were with Christie.

Christie, satisfied she had as many people as she could get under her banner, moved to the gate of the cage and watched Marsha be led across the warehouse floor. A few times Marsha was lost from view and when she was gone for more than minute, she then reappeared when she was led up the metal staircase.

The three ghouls remained at the bottom, their rifles across their chests like soldiers on guard. Marsha climbed the metal steps with a dull ache in her heart. Seth waited for her at the top, and as she gazed up at him, she tried to see the man she once knew. The jaw was the same, as was the hair, the build somewhat smaller now that Seth had become a zombie. But she could still see a resemblance to the man she had loved.

When she reached the top, Jonah/Seth gazed down at her. He reached out and touched her cheek, then pulled the hand away, holding his arm out and over the metal railing.

Making a fist, he raised his thumb for all the ghouls to see.

Immediately, a low pitched moan filled the warehouse, the zombies knowing it was time to feed again.

Jonah then pointed to the cage Marsha was in, and the ghouls went to it, opening the gate and entering.

Marsha gasped when it was Christie who was picked to be the next victim in the death circle. The policewoman fought like a banshee, kicking and screaming, but there were too many zombies holding her for her to escape, and even if she did, she would only be run down a second later. But the woman never stopped fighting, and a minute later was tossed into the scarlet circle. She immediately slid in the gore and offal, slipping and falling heavily to the floor. Her entire left side was now coated in gobbets of flesh and a large piece of someone's skin adhered to her hip. Brushing it off with a face filled with disgust, she spun around, staring at the ghouls as they moaned and wailed at her. They were only waiting for Jonah to signal they could feed; his dominance over his undead brethren all but complete.

Marsha gasped when she saw her friend thrown into the circle and she turned to Jonah, her eyes wide in fear.

"No, Seth, please, not her, no more. How can you do this to people? You were once so kind. This has to stop," she pleaded.

Seth turned and gazed down at her. He had a good four inches on her and she remembered staring up into his deep blue eyes, lost in the azure orbs that seemed to swirl like a galaxy of stars. But now all she saw was emptiness. It was then that she realized the man she had loved was no more, that though this figure in front of her resembled her lost love, in truth her love was dead, and this foul shell of a man was evil incarnate.

Seth turned away from her then and he raised his arm higher, then he turned his thumb down to the floor and the ghouls wailed in what seemed to resemble happiness. They charged into the circle and Christie found herself fighting for her life, a fight she could never win. She punched and kicked at the hands and faces that got in front of her, but as she bashed the ones in front of her, more came up from behind, pale dry hands wrapping around her neck and teeth sinking into her thighs and lower legs.

She screamed from the pain, but still she fought on. Her right fist pummeled a nose, sending crushed cartilage into a brain, another she kicked in the balls, the dried up sacks of testicles flattening to dust as her foot cracked pelvis bone. Her left elbow came up and back, dislocating a jaw on a ghoul who got too close, the jaw sagging like a wet paper bag, useless. Her left fingers, the nails sharp, plucked out an eye, squeezing the orb within her palm as she fought tooth and nail for one more second of life. But though she battled like a warrior of old, there were simply too many bodies for her to overcome. Soon, hands had her from all sides and she was brought to the blood-lathered floor. She shrieked then, long and loud, but now with pain but with anger at losing her fight. When the first set of teeth to find her torso sank deep, a crimson pool of blood appeared as the ghoul pulled back its head, a juicy vermilion morsel now in its jaws.

Marsha was in tears now, the scene below becoming blurry as she watched Christie forced to the floor. Then, through the shifting bodies, Christie's eyes found hers from across the warehouse.

"Marsha, do it, goddammit! You have to or everyone's gonna die!" Christie yelled, her words morphing to screams of pain. She wanted to say more to Marsha, but instead of words, she choked up a bloody froth that sprayed a ghoul's face. Her eyes took on a far away look then as her insides were torn out piece by bloody piece.

Marsha watched in horror as her friend was dissected and she felt her stomach rumble inside her with sickness. Her knees were weak and she felt like she was going to go insane. So much death and pain, and for what?

Shaking her head, she turned to gaze up at Jonah, while below, Christie's body parts were divvied up and fed upon, the ghouls feasting merrily.

"No, she's right, this has got to stop, Seth, this can't keep going on."

Seth gazed down at her, not seeming to understand what Marsha was saying. Marsha looked into those white, dead eyes one last time, hoping, no praying, there was one last ounce of humanity still left in there, something that would cause her to pause.

But there was none, and with the anger and grief of her lost friend still fresh in her mind, she reached inside her shirt with her left hand and pulled out the knitting needle.

From the warehouse floor below, all eyes were on Marsha and Jonah on the balcony, and every human in the warehouse watched as Marsha stretched her arm out to its furthest point and then brought up the knitting needle in a wide arc, the target, Jonah's right ear.

The tip of the needle was sharp, and Marsha used all her strength behind the blow, the needle sinking deep, puncturing eardrum and continuing into the brain within.

Jonah's eyes went wide in shock as the tip pierced his brain. Instinctively, he reached out and wrapped both hands around Marsha's throat, the two seeming to be locked in a lover's embrace.

Marsha remembered what Christie had said and she twisted the needle, the tip slicing brain matter like it was pudding. Jonah/Seth opened his mouth and roared his pain, his hands squeezing tighter around her throat. His fingers compressed her carotid arteries and she began to feel lightheaded, but her resolve was firm and still she twisted, mashing his brain to bite-sized chunks within in his skull.

The two seemed to remain locked in an embrace for an eternity, but in reality no more than thirty seconds had passed, but when Marsha had severed enough brain matter to kill her former lover, Jonah's eyes flared wide and he opened his mouth. He tired to speak one last time, his rotting vocal cords all but gone, but he managed one word.

"Marsha..." He croaked.

Marsha's own eyes went wide though she was on the verge of losing consciousnesses at hearing him utter her name. Regret filled her and she pulled her hand back, the bloody tip of the needle spraying gore out and over the balcony, the drops of blood falling to the floor below. And then Seth/Jonah died, toppling over the balcony.

Marsha lost consciousness at the same moment, and with Seth's hands still wrapped around her neck in a deathly embrace, she felt gravity pull her down as she fell into a deep dark void she would never awaken from.

A gasp filled the warehouse as the human prisoners watched the two bodies topple over the railing and fall to the hard, concrete floor below.

Marsha's unconscious form was first, her head hitting the floor, followed immediately by her body. The force of the fall was so great her skull cracked like a rotten melon, her brains spilling out to paint the concrete pink and red, Seth fell on top of her, his arms seeming to drape over hers. One of Marsha's arms bounced after landing and it wrapped around Seth's body, the two entwined in death forever.

All around the two shattered bodies, the zombies stood motionless.

Their leader was gone and they were without a ruler. Some stared at the floor while others stared at each other. Even the more intelligent ones knew not what to do. They had been awakened by Jonah and he had told them what to do. Even with the modicum of intelligence they had no purpose, no true drive to do anything other than feed.

But while the zombies stood still, not understanding what had happened, the humans were filled with hope.

As one massive crowd, more than half the occupants of the cage Christie and Marsha had been in took this as their last and final chance to escape.

With a mighty roar they surged forward and crashed into the gate of their cage, knocking the zombies out of the way as they poured into the warehouse. When those humans did this, the other cages filled with humanity saw what was happening and quickly rallied around each other, pushing out of their cages and hopefully to freedom. Fists, legs and hands began battering the ghouls, women jumping onto backs and screaming as they took out their rage and frustration on the animated corpses that had imprisoned them and killed their loved ones.

In less than a minute, the warehouse was a seething cauldron of fighting humanity as the last vestiges of the city's population fought to live beyond the next five minutes.

But then the zombies snapped out of whatever stupor they had fallen under and soon ghoul and human alike were battling for dominion over the other. The old man Marsha and Christie had first met was brought down by five zombies who tore him apart while the tall man with the filthy shirt was dragged under ten more decaying attackers, his screams of pain filling the warehouse. But the ghouls took casualties, too. One zombie was knocked to the floor and its head was twisted clean off like a cork, then tossed away like a beach ball. Another ghoul was grabbed from all sides and was drawn and quartered, the four angry men each holding a limb.

One man held a severed arm and he used it like a club as he swung it at approaching zombies.

Blood was an inch deep on the floor, body parts everywhere, as the humans fought for their right to exist.

Ten minutes and the battle still raged on, the humans suffering catastrophic losses simply because they were outnumbered twenty to one.

The zombies were now unfettered by Jonah and they fed like wild animals, tearing into the warm flesh of the humans with abandon.

They fed like ravenous dogs, shoving the warm meat into their mouths as fast as they were able.

Then, as the battle raged, one human, clear of the fighting for a few seconds, heard what sounded like a high whistling coming from overhead.

Glancing up to the ceiling, the man's eyes creased in curiosity, wondering what that sound could be.

Then his thoughts were irrelevant as he was jumped by three ghouls, who forced him to the floor and ripped his throat out, a geyser of blood dancing in the air to fall back to the earth.

The whistling grew louder and seemed to override the battle within the warehouse, but no one paid it any mind. The danger was in front of them, and all the humans knew they had to kill as many zombies as possible if they ever hoped to escape the building.

Then the whistling stopped, and a thunderclap filled the warehouse, seeming to absorb all light and sound.

In the blink of an eye, every human fighting for his or her life, and every zombie, was incinerated in a blinding flash of yellow light.

The battle had been decided, and neither side would win.

Chapter 23

A quarter mile off shore from the warehouse, a United States Naval Destroyer was anchored, facing inland. On the bridge, while more than a dozen crewmen went about the business of running the ship, the captain stood at the main windshield, a pair of black binoculars in his hands.

Reflected in the glass of the binoculars was the orange and red mushroom cloud of the explosion that had just leveled the warehouse. The man watched as a ball of flame five hundred feet high burned with the intensity of a small sun. He had been told napalm had been used along with conventional weaponry.

The warehouse, full of what could only be called *sentient zombies*, had become too much of a risk. For some reason all the ghouls had gathered in one place, this after laying waste to the city and taking every man, woman and child back to the building.

Those humans that had remained behind had been torn limb from limb, their flesh feasted on like wild dogs had gotten to them.

Whatever had happened in this city could not be allowed to spread across the rest of the Untied States. So the President had authorized the use of extreme force, even the trapped humans inside considered expendable.

Collateral damage was the preferred term.

The Captain watched as the jet which had dropped the bomb soared off into the sky, leaving behind a raging inferno that consumed everything within a quarter mile of the docks. Though the initial blast had died down, secondary explosions continued one after the other, blasting the warehouse to pieces and hurling chunks of steel and flaming sections of cement into the air in all directions.

The underground gas main had caught fire, and though the men on the perimeter had cut off the source, there was still gas in the lines below the foundation of the warehouse. But the Captain knew the fires would die down eventually.

Already he could see military helicopters flying over the blast zone, searching for any survivors. Not that they would be allowed to live, of course.

No one could know what had happened here today. If the uprising of zombies was ever made public, all across the United States normal citizens wouldn't allow the slave ghouls to be around them. Without the zombies to do all the menial tasks needed to run civilization, the way of life the population of the United States enjoyed would disappear forever. He knew he didn't want that.

Even on his ship he had more than fifty zombies. They did everything from cleaning the bilges to scraping paint to mopping the decks. If it wasn't for the ghouls, he would be hard pressed to keep his ship afloat. Even five years later, more than half of the United States Navy's ships were still mothballed due to lack of manpower to run them.

No, the zombies were needed to do these chores or the world would all be thrown back into the 1800's, at least for a generation. Hopefully, in the next twenty years or so there would be a new generation of people to take the reins from the survivors of the plague. When the children now born, and the ones born in the past few years, were old enough, they would have more jobs than they could handle waiting for them.

That was why the mandate for all married couples to have a minimum of five or more children was passed. For the country to grow, its people had to be born again.

He could hear the radio chatter on the broadband as the helicopters talked back and forth to one another. So far no survivors had been found.

The captain nodded; pleased the op had gone as planned. It had been a tactical decision to try and wipe out all the zombies in one swoop, and it looked like it had paid off wonderfully.

Next to the Captain, staring out the windshield, an ensign could see the large black cloud of billowing smoke as it filled the sky.

"I can't help but wonder if this was really necessary," the ensign said more to himself than to the captain. "After all, all those living people have just been killed. There were over two hundred heat signatures in that warehouse. And now they're dead. We just killed American citizens, sir. Isn't that who we're supposed to be protecting?"

The captain nodded, knowing exactly what the ensign meant. He had been as naïve as this young man many years ago, but after living through the plague, he had become a much stronger man than he once was. At the time of the plague, this man next to him had been only eleven. Now at sixteen he had been rushed into military service, as most teenagers were. The new age for serving in the military was sixteen due once again to lack of manpower. He had heard even stories of many men being allowed in at fourteen if they were big enough and passed the exams.

"They're collateral damage, son," the captain said. "I know it's hard to accept it, but we had no choice. If we went in there with ground troops some of those deadheads could have gotten away. No, son, we needed to get them all at once without them expecting it." He shook his head. "It's a shame we had to sacrifice so many good people, but it's for the greater good. They're all heroes now."

"The greater good, sir?"

The captain nodded, lowering the binoculars.

"Yes, son, we need to keep what happened here today quiet. If word got out about sentient deadheads, well, I'm sure you can imagine what that would do to our economy. Besides, what ever happened here was some kind of fluke. Nowhere else in the country has there been a report of an incident like this. And now that we've destroyed the nest, so to speak, whatever happened here is over. Once we deal with the news media, tell them this was an outbreak, a small resurgence of the plague perhaps, or a chemical spill that had to be burned to be sanitized, everything will go back to normal."

"But, sir, everyone knows the plague's been destroyed," the ensign said.

"Maybe, son, maybe, but fear is a powerful thing. If you remind people of what might happen, no matter how farfetched or improbable, every once in a while it keeps them at your mercy." He grinned like a father to a son then. "I know it sounds harsh, Ensign, but sometimes the American people need to be treated like children, it's always been like this; ever since the U.S. government was first formed two hundred years ago."

The ensign gazed out the main window at the pall of smoke, his mouth sliding into a frown.

"But, sir, don't the American people have a right to know what really happened here today?"

The captain grinned then, setting down the binoculars so he could look the ensign in the eye, ignoring the large inferno that had once been a warehouse filled with people.

"No, son, they don't. What they do have is a right to be told what we want to tell them. Now go radio the troops on land and find out when they'll be ready to get in there and do a thorough sanitization of the area. After all, the damn deadheads are dead; it's still possible a few could escape the flames."

"Yes, sir," the ensign said, saluted and moved off.

"Oh, and son, make sure you get an exact eta. We can't spare one extra moment than we have to. There's already been a few news helicopters sniffing around. They've been chased away, but those media bastards don't give up easy."

The ensign nodded and rushed off while the captain turned back to the windshield and gazed out at the smoke, the bridge a hive of activity around him.

The ensign came back five minutes later with a sheet of paper in his hand.

"Captain, the ground troops will be ready to move in within the hour. They say it's still too hot for them to go in just yet, even with their fire retardant suits."

"Very good, son, I guess we'll have to wait then," the captain said as he picked up the binoculars again and watched the flames lick the sky like angry demons.

Another crewman appeared from a side door, just off the bridge, his insignia on his shirt stating he was a radioman.

"Sir, I have an urgent call from the President. He wants an update," the radioman said.

The caption nodded, lowered the binoculars and handed then to the ensign, patting the younger man's shoulder in the process.

"Don't worry, son, we'll get this shit cleaned up, tell the media some bullshit and then everything will go back to normal, just like it always does after a disaster. In history this will be nothing but a fleck of dust on the white sheet of our great country." Turning, he walked off the bridge, the XO taking over with a wave to the caption.

The ensign raised the binoculars to his eyes and stared at the flames as they burned brightly, the orange and yellow tendrils looking like a living entity. It was still a shame, all those people just snuffed out like they had never been born. No one would ever even know who had been in there, even the bones that escaped the fire soon to be destroyed. He couldn't help but wonder what exactly had happened in this city to cause the deadheads to begin to think.

And could it happen again?"

Shaking his head, he decided, no, it couldn't. It was impossible, whatever had happened here had been a fluke, a one in a million incident. The odds of it happening again were probably ridiculously high.

He nodded to himself, knowing the captain was right. He was a great man and the ensign respected him immensely.

Give it a few weeks and no one will even remember what had happened here today.

The American people had very short attention spans, and whether he liked it or not, that attention span seemed to get shorter with each passing year.

Epilogue

Three months later, about a mile outside of Pittsburgh, Pennsylvania, a zombie named Ceasar worked on the quarter acre of land owned by his master. The name Ceasar wasn't his true name of course, but when this particular zombie had finished his indoctrination and rudimentarily learning and had to be released into the work force, it took the name his handler had bestowed upon him.

The handler had been a history buff, especially about Rome and the time of Julius Ceasar. So when it had been time to name this ghoul, the handler had chosen the name from history, seeing no particular significance to it other than a way to separate this ghoul from the others in training.

While Ceasar cut the hedges lining his owner's land with the neighbor's, he found himself becoming distracted by a family of squirrels playing in a nearby tree. Without realizing it, Ceasar let his newly sharpened hedge clippers droop to his side as he stared at the squirrels playing tag. A wan smile creased his dry, dead lips as the hollow echo of a memory form a past life plucked at his dead brain stem, tantalizing close and yet still frustratingly out of reach.

As he watched the squirrels, he never moved when the sprinkler came on, the water droplets raining down on him, covering him in a fine sheen of moisture and plastering his hair to his scalp.

While Ceasar watched the squirrels play, lost in reverie, his owner glanced up from the newspaper he was reading across the wide, green manicured lawn.

The newspaper was in his hands and a half can of beer sat with condensation on it on a small yard table next to him. He had just finished reading about how it was the three month anniversary of the airplane that had crashed into the waterfront across the country and how experimental chemicals the plane had been carrying in its cargo hold had spread across the city, causing a massive death count that wiped out the entire population in the blink of an eye.

There had been weeks of mourning over the terrible tragedy, but in the past two weeks the news coverage had dwindled. In another few weeks there would be barely a mention of it as other, more newsworthy items took top billing.

The owner, a tall thin man in his late fifties with a receding hairline and the name of Charles Montgomery the third, glanced over the top of his newspaper to see his zombie wasn't working. As he stared at the ghoul, he realized Ceasar was watching something he couldn't see from where he was sitting.

Grumbling about the damn deadheads, Charles leaned over and picked up the cattle prod which was standard issue for all trained zombies. As the dead felt no pain, sometimes the cattle prods were all that got them moving. And Charles had been having some mild trouble lately with his zombie. For no apparent reason he would catch his ghoul just staring at an object, like it was thinking about something.

And that was impossible because it was dead, a zombie, only able to do the most basic tasks and lately even those were becoming unmanageable.

So with a stern look on his face, Charles stood up with cattle prod in hand and crossed the lawn to Ceasar. As he got closer and realized Ceasar was watching squirrels of all things, his ire grew even more.

He was already formulating the complaint letter he was planning on e-mailing to the company who supplied the ghoul workers in the morning, hoping he could get another one, and perhaps a discount to boot for his aggravation in having to change out the one he already had.

To reach Ceasar, Charles had to walk through the sprinkler, and his anger grew even more as his clothing began to get wet.

Great, now he had to change, he thought.

He was so angry by the time he reached Ceasar he wanted to lash out at anything, even at a zombie that felt no pain. Deciding he needed to inflict as much pain as he could, he lifted his arms and jabbed the cattle prod into the back of Ceasar's head, deciding he might get a better result there as when he would shock the torso in past times he barely got a nudge out of the ghoul.

Perhaps if he'd read the manual that had come with Ceasar, he may have given that idea a second thought, but he didn't, so he did, and the voltage shot through the tip of the prod and into Ceasar's gray matter, flooding his dead brain with electricity as the zombie danced a jig on the lawn, the hedge clippers falling point first from his hand to stick in grass like a lawn dart.

A second later, Ceasar fell to the wet grass, his white eyes staring up at the sky as his brain sizzled with electricity.

Charles' lips curved into a sneer as he stared at his property twitching in the wet grass.

"Now get back to work, you rotting pile of shit," Charles snapped. "I paid good money for you and I expect you to do the shit you're supposed to do. If I have to come back again you'll really see how bad it can get."

Feeling satisfied now that he had vented his anger, he turned away from Ceasar to go back to his beer and paper.

As he walked away, he didn't bother to cast a glance back at Ceasar who was even now slowly getting to his feet again. The ghoul reached over and pulled the hedge clippers from the lawn, then turned and began walking after his owner, moving as fast as his stiff legs would allow. But it was more than enough as Charles wasn't in a rush, and he was strolling casually away, the cattle prod swinging from his right hand while he walked.

If Charles had bothered to take one final look over his shoulder, he would have seen his property coming at him, the hedge clippers held high in preparation of a killing blow.

If Charles had bothered to look over his shoulder in the last few seconds he had left alive on this earth, he would have seen a spark of intelligence in the white, cold eyes of Ceasar that hadn't been there before.

The revolution wasn't over.

In fact, it had only just begun.

The following is a bonus,
short story from the author

Going Up?

Paul Francis paused as he walked through the massive foyer while on his way to the bank of elevators in the high-rise building in the middle of Manhattan.

All around him were the signs of life as people moved about on their daily errands. The high-rise was filled with the offices of lawyers, doctors and a hundred other occupations, all wrapped up in sixty floors of steel and stone.

And it was all his.

Paul Francis was one of the richest men in New York.

He had made his first million by the age of twenty two and had cleared a net of five million plus by the time he was twenty five.

Of course, that was more than twenty years ago.

Now Paul was in his early forties and he planned on living another fifty if he had his way.

Though not an evil man, Paul had done his share of distasteful things in his life and had been so focused on making money he had become somewhat of a hermit.

While not an angel, as no one who had managed to amass the fortune he had could be, and he had broken the rules now and then, he still considered himself to be a good man.

The only thing that plagued him was how alone he was in this world he had created for himself. Though a wealthy man, he had no one to share it with. His parents had died many years ago, both victims of a variety of ailments.

So, though Paul had more money than he knew what to do with, in truth, he wasn't necessarily a happy man. The spark he once had, that thrill of life, had long ago left him, like smoke caught in a gentle updraft. He'd tried many things to jump start his will to live, but none had taken affect on him.

With a weary sigh, he began walking again, his destination his private elevator which would take him to the top floor of the high-rise. From there he could gaze out on the majestic beauty of New York and imagine how it would all be his some day.

Upon reaching the elevators, he frowned deeply when he saw his private elevator was open, a man in an engineer's uniform crouched inside. The man's tools were spread out around him and a small yellow sign hung near the bottom, warning others the elevator was out of service, which was silly.

After all, the elevator was only for him, and no one else could use the lift to his office and private sanctuary.

Stepping closer, Paul leaned over the man's shoulder while the engineer played with the control panel in the elevator.

"Ah, excuse me, are you almost done? I wanted to get up to my office," Paul said with a slight grin. He may be rich, but he still knew of the common courtesy all humans deserved. He hadn't fallen so far into stagnation that he wasn't a polite soul.

The engineer turned around, setting his screwdriver down so he could look up into Paul's face. He was a plain man with a balding pate and small eyes. Laugh lines as well as a few wrinkles were scattered about the pleasant visage.

"I'll be finished in a sec', Mr. Francis. Sorry to keep you waiting," the engineer said in a subservient tone.

Paul checked his watch, his impatience getting the better of him. The thing was, he really wasn't in a rush. Once he reached his office, he merely planned on twirling his thumbs while his corporation rolled onward. He had created such a massive machine; he truly believed it would go on forever, long after he was dead and gone from this mortal coil. But of course that wouldn't be for a long, long time.

"Fine, fine, I have a few calls to make. I'll just wait over here," Paul told the engineer as he pulled out his cell phone.

The engineer nodded, picked up his screwdriver and got back to work. As for Paul, he did make a call or two but they were really not that important. He let others handle the complexities of running his business now and found he had more idle time to waste his life with nowadays.

The public elevators opened and closed, children, adults, and parents looking harried, all coming and going to their private destinations. Ten minutes later, the engineer waved to Paul, getting his attention.

"All set, Mr. Francis, but I think I should ride up with you just to make sure everything's working properly."

"Fine, fine, whatever, just as long as you're done," Paul said with a touch of impatience in his voice.

The engineer took a step back, gathered his tools, and Paul entered the elevator, the engineer following with a smile.

Paul used his key card and slid it into the slot, this allowing him access to the top floor. The polished stainless steel doors closed and the elevator began its ascent.

Paul looked down at his shoes, checking to see if they had received any smudges on his walk through the building. He had recently had them shined and took great pride in the thousand dollar loafers.

When you were rich, money was plentiful, so it meant nothing, merely a means to an end.

It was when he looked back up and caught the engineer's reflection in the elevator doors that his heart seemed to stop in his chest and his blood began to run cold. His breath lodged in his throat, his mouth opening slightly, no words escaping.

Instead of seeing the reflection of the plain man in an engineer's uniform, Paul stared at the visage of Death incarnate.

The figure was now seven feet tall, the top if its head scraping the ceiling of the elevator. A dark black cloak shrouded the figure in darkness, and when the form shifted, Paul could see just the hint of white, like a skull, from where the visage of a human face should be. Two red dots glowed where eyes would have been on a face, and Paul felt his bowels wanting to let go, only his willpower stopping him from soiling himself.

The figure's hands were the most unsettling.

Skeletal, bleached-white fingers held onto the elevator railing, the figure leaning back as any casual rider would, as the elevator shot upwards to what could feel like Heaven, the tall building like a spire in the sky.

Paul said nothing, the figure watching the control panel, eyeing the electrics to make sure everything was working properly.

Paul blinked his eyes, squeezing them closed; telling himself what he was seeing was impossible. It had to be, because the reality would be far too much to contemplate.

After all, why would Death himself be standing behind him if he wasn't about to die?

The chilling figure had come to harvest his soul, and Paul felt utterly helpless as he gazed into those glowing red eyes.

His forehead began to sweat and he could feel dampness under his arms. His heart had begun beating again, but now it was like he had his own personal drum solo in his chest.

The entire time, Death never moved, never wavered, only stood behind him, staring at the elevator panel.

As the elevator shot upwards to the top of the building, Paul reflected on his life, how he had lost his way.

Sure, he had money, but what had he done with it to truly help others? He could easily spend half of what he'd earned on others and he would have never, ever felt the loss financially.

One time, his father had told him how greedy man was and how he would always want more, even when he had his fill. How man was a glutton, and could have enough food and money to last three lifetimes and yet the greed inside would still want more, even if that meant others would suffer.

Paul reflected on all that now as he stared at the grim visage of Death and waited for that bone-white finger to come down on his shoulder, taking his soul to whatever world came next.

And what would come next?

He had been a devout Catholic his entire life, but now? When death was literally at his door, so to speak, he couldn't help but wonder if all he had been taught, all he had believed, was nothing but crap.

But then, if that was so, how could this entity exist at all?

The numbers flashed by on the elevator panel, and Paul sensed that when the elevator reached the top floor, so too would the end of his life.

He found himself full of regrets; of wishing he had done things differently.

He realized if he had only had a second chance, he would do things so very, very differently. He could start a few charity organizations, and other human related charities that could help with the betterment of mankind.

And most of all, he would find someone to love him, as he would her. They could start a family and he could remember what is was like to be alive, not so wrapped up in work and greed that he forgot about the simpler things in life; the things that connect us all and make us one.

Paul realized at that moment in time he would do things so very differently if he had the chance.

But it was now too late.

The elevator was slowing, the numbers ticking by as it approached the top floor. Behind him, Death shifted his weight, and Paul knew the hand would be coming down on his shoulder and he would feel...what? A blackness? A void? What would happen?

He didn't want to know, he knew that with all his heart.

He felt faint now, his shirt filled with perspiration and making his flesh sticky under his tailor made jacket. His legs felt weak and he just wanted to sit down, right on the floor of the elevator.

He could feel tears welling up in his eyes and he tried to fight them back, wanting to at least go out like a man, with a modicum of pride and courage.

The elevator stopped with a gentle nudge, so soft it would be ignored by all but the most perceptive of people. But Paul was perceptive and he found at this moment in his life, when he was about to die, his nerve endings and impulses were filled with fire for wanting to live!

Why now, when he was about to die, did he realize how much he wanted to live? Why had he squandered so much of the precious gift of life when it was with him and only now that he was losing it did he realize what he'd had?

The doors opened with a soft chime and the engineer grinned, nodding to himself.

Paul waited, knowing what was coming and helpless to stop it.

"Well, Mr. Francis, aren't you going to leave? The engineer asked.

Paul said nothing for almost ten seconds, only his beating heart filling the void of silence, then he managed to utter a few words, the tone sounding like a five-year-old's.

"Aren't... aren't you going to take me? Isn't it my time?"

The figure leaned forward slightly and Paul was now able to see into that void where a face should be. The dark red eyes were floating in what seemed the air, a glimpse of a skull flashing like a strobe light, and below them nothing but darkness.

Deep, ebony darkness that seemed to go on forever.

"Do you want it to be your time, Mr. Francis?"

Paul managed to shake his head back and forth, not fully understanding what he was being asked, but knowing the answer was no.

"Fair enough, then," Death replied.

Death moved past him, and out into the hallway, then turned and gazed back at Paul with those crimson eyes.

"It looks like your elevator is all set, Mr. Francis. It was just a short in the control panel. It's all fixed now."

Paul's mouth slid open and he looked like a bug catcher.

"But what about...?

"What about what? What about taking you with me?"

Paul nodded, his mouth still open.

The engineer waved his hand in front of him idly, like someone does when they don't believe what you are telling them is true.

"I'm not here for you, Mr. Francis. I'm just working my day job. Even Death has to eat, you know. You shouldn't have been able to see through my guise. You're quite a perceptive man, Mr. Francis, more so than most people I interact with." There was a blurring and then the visage of Death was gone and only the engineer remained.

The engineer shrugged. "Well, take care and make sure that elevator gets scheduled maintenance."

Paul nodded again as he watched Death stroll away across the hallway. The figure transformed back into Death for a brief moment and then back to the engineer again, and Paul stared as the man with the bag of tools headed for the opposite bank of elevators from him.

The engineer pressed the call button and tapped his shoe while he waited, Paul watching the entire time, dumbstruck.

The chime signaled the car's arrival, the doors opened and the engineer stepped inside, a subtle wave to Paul as he entered.

"Be seeing you," the engineer said with a knowing grin that spoke volumes and nothing at the same time.

Then the doors hissed closed and the figure was gone.

Paul stood perfectly still, staring out through the elevator doors and into the carpeted hallway with its thousand dollar light fixtures and paintings adorning the walls. He didn't move for the next ten minutes.

But slowly, in time, his heart slowed, his mouth closed, and his perspiring stopped.

Blinking his eyes clear, he finally made himself move, stepping into the hallway. The doors slid closed behind him and he stared off to his office door at the end.

He still didn't understand what had just happened to him, but he felt like he had just been pardoned by God Himself.

For some reason he was still here and he realized what a truly wonderful gift he'd just received.

He was now able to make good on all those regrets he'd made only minutes ago.

With a bounce to his step, he headed off to his office. He had a lot of calls to make and knew he would be very busy for the next few months, but that was okay, as he knew he would be enjoying every second of it.

Something had changed inside him and he now felt alive, more alive than he had in years.

It was good to be alive, and if he could help it, he would stay that way for a long time to come, and he would do it by appreciating every moment he had on God's green Earth.

Notes from the author

Hi, and welcome to one of my ruminations on life, love and the fate of the world.

This time I'm going to share something a little personal with you.

It's about book reviews and the like on Amazon, Barnes and Noble, and on all the websites devoted to zombies and stuff.

At the time of writing this I was lucky enough to get a great review for the book *The Rage Plague.*

After reading this review I felt great, I was proud for many reasons, one being that I had created a piece of artwork from nothing and had then been able to let other people enjoy it.

But no sooner did this happen then I received a bad review for one of my other books.

Now just getting a bad review isn't the end of the world, right? After all, there are so many different kinds of people out in the world, with different ideas of what they like and dislike, that the odds there will be people who read my work and don't like it is a given.

But this review was something more. This reviewer seemed to attack me personally for no other reason than because I am a self-published author, as if that was a bad word or something.

So here I was, supposed to feel great 'cause I had this great review for *Rage Plague,* but all I could think about was this guy's bad review.

Sure, I should have gotten over it, but ask any writer and they will tell you it's hard not to dwell on the bad ones.

But isn't that human nature?

Think about all the great things that have happened to you in your life, and then the bad ones. Why is it we, as human beings, seem to only be happy for a short period of time about the good stuff, taking it for granted, but when something bad happens, even if it isn't that bad to begin with, we dwell on it till the cows come home.

So, what I'm trying to say in my convoluted way is that whether you like a book, movie or painting, or didn't, always remember that book, movie or painting was nothing, it didn't exist until someone with the talent, the will, and the drive to create it did so.

And that at the end of the book, movie, painting, and statues too, there is a human being with hopes, feelings and dreams the same as yourself.

So the next time you pick up a book, even if you don't like it, always remember what it truly took to create that work of art in your hands.

And by doing so, you just might appreciate how truly amazing it really is.

Anthony Giangregorio
March 2009

DEAD RECKONING: DAWNING OF THE DEAD
By Anthony Giangregorio

THE DEAD HAVE RISEN!

In the dead city of Pittsburgh, two small enclaves struggle to survive, eking out an existence of hand to mouth.

But instead of working together, both groups battle for the last remaining fuel and supplies of a city filled with the living dead.

Six months after the initial outbreak, a lone helicopter arrives bearing two more survivors and a newborn baby. One enclave welcomes them, while the other schemes to steal their helicopter and escape the decaying city.

With no police, fire, or social services existing, the two will battle for dominance in the steel city of the walking dead.

But when the dust settles, the question is: will the remaining humans be the winners, or the losers?

When the dead walk, the line between Heaven and Hell is so twisted and bent there is no line at all.

RISE OF THE DEAD
By Anthony Giangregorio

DEATH IS ONLY THE BEGINNING

In less than forty-eight hours, more than half the globe was infected.
In another forty-eight, the rest would be enveloped.
The reason?
A science experiment gone horribly wrong which enabled the dead to walk, their flesh rotting on their bones even as they seek human prey.

Jeremy was an ordinary nineteen year old slacker. He partied too much and had done poorly in high school. After a night of drinking and drugs, he awoke to find the world a very different place from the one he'd left the night before.

The dead were walking and feeding on the living, and as Jeremy stepped out into a world gone mad, the dead spotting him alone and unarmed in the middle of the street, he had to wonder if he would live long enough to see his twentieth birthday.

ANOTHER EXCITING CHAPTER IN THE DEADWATER SERIES!

BOOK 6

DEAD UNION

By Anthony Giangregorio

BRAVE NEW WORLD

More than a year has passed since the world died not with a bang, but with a moan.
Where sprawling cities once stood, now only the dead inhabit the hollow walls of a shattered civilization; a mockery of lives once led.
But there are still survivors in this barren world, all slowly struggling to take back what was stripped from their birthright; the promise of a world free of the undead.
Fortified towns have shunned the outside world, becoming massive fortresses in their own right. These refugees of a world torn asunder are once again trying to carve out a new piece of the earth, or hold onto what little they already possess.

HOSTAGES

Henry Watson and his warrior survivalists are conscripted by a mad colonel, one of the last military leaders still functioning in the decimated United States. The colonel has settled in Fort Knox, and from there plans to rule the world with his slave army of lost souls and the last remaining soldiers of a defunct army.
But first he must take back America and mold it in his own image; and he will crush all who oppose him, including the new recruits of Henry and crew.
The battle lines are drawn with the fate of America at stake, and this time, the outcome may be unsure.
In a world where the dead walk, even the grave isn't safe.

THE DARK
By Anthony Giangregorio

DARKNESS FALLS

The darkness came without warning.
First New York, then the rest of United States, and then the world became enveloped in a perpetual night without end.
With no sunlight, eventually the planet will wither and die, bringing on a new Ice Age. But that isn't problem for the human race, for humanity will be dead long before that happens.
There is something in the dark, creatures only seen in nightmares, and they are on the prowl.
Evolution has changed and man is no longer the dominant species.
When we are children, we are told not to fear the dark, that what we believe to exist in the shadows is false.
Unfortunately, that is no longer true.

ANOTHER EXCITING CHAPTER IN THE DEADWATER SERIES!

Book 2

DEADRAIN
By Anthony Giangregorio

Welcome to the New America, population: 0

When a bacterial outbreak contaminates America's lower atmosphere, the resulting rain mutates into a deadly conduit for death.

Human's all over America are exposed and within a matter of days society has crumbled and the walking dead rule the land.

The America we know is gone, replaced by a new order; where the dead walk and humans are the prey.

Henry Watson and his small group of companions travel the country, searching for someplace better, someplace where the rain is safe.

In the New America the rules have changed; survive or perish.

DARK PLACES
By Anthony Giangregorio

A cave-in inside the Boston subway unleashes something that should have stayed buried forever.

Three boys sneak out to a haunted junkyard after dark and find more than they gambled on.

In a world where everyone over twelve has died from a mysterious illness, one young boy tries to carry on.

A mysterious man in black tries his hand at a game of chance at a local carnival, to interesting results.

God, Allah, and Buddha play a friendly game of poker with the fate of the Earth resting in the balance.

Ever have one of those days where everything that can go wrong, does? Well, so did Byron, and no one should have a day like this!

Thad had an imaginary friend named Charlie when he was a child. Charlie would make him do bad things. Now Thad is all grown up and guess who's coming for a visit?

These and other short stories, all filled with frozen moments of dread and wonder, will keep you captivated long into the night.

Just be sure to watch out when you turn off the light!

DEAD RAGE
By Anthony Giangregorio

An unknown virus spreads across the globe, turning ordinary people into bloodthirsty, ravenous killers.

Only a small percentage of the population is immune and soon become prey to the infected.

Amongst the infected comes a man, stricken by the virus, yet still retaining his grasp on reality. His need to destroy the *normals* becomes an obsession and he raises an army of killers to seek out and kill all who aren't *changed* like himself.

A few survivors gather together on the outskirts of Chicago and find themselves running for their lives as the specter of death looms over all.

The Dead Rage virus will find you, no matter where you hide.

Also available as The Rage Plague by Permuted Press.

THE MONSTER UNDER THE BED
By Anthony Giangregorio

Rupert was just one of many monsters that inhabit the human world, scaring children before bed. Only Rupert wanted to play with the children he was forced to scare.

When Rupert meets Timmy, an instant friendship is born. Running away from his abusive step-father, Timmy leaves home, embarking on a journey that leads him to New York City.

On his way, Timmy will realize that the true monsters are other adults who are just waiting to take advantage of a small boy, all alone in the big city.

Can Rupert save him?

Or will Timmy just become another statistic.

SOULEATER
By Anthony Giangregorio

Twenty years ago, Jason Lawson witnessed the brutal death of his father by something only seen in nightmares, something so horrible he'd blocked it from his mind.

Now twenty years later the creature is back, this time for his son.

Jason won't let that happen.

He'll travel to the demon's world, struggling every second to rescue his son from its clutches.

But what he doesn't know is that the portal will only be open for a finite time and if he doesn't return with his son before it closes, then he'll be trapped in the demon's dimension forever.

DEAD TALES: SHORT STORIES TO DIE FOR
By Anthony Giangregorio

In a world much like our own, terrorists unleash a deadly dis-ease that turns people into flesh-eating ghouls.

A camping trip goes horribly wrong when forces of evil seek to dominate mankind.

After losing his life, a man returns reincarnated again and again; his soul inhabiting the bodies of animals.

In the Colorado Mountains, a woman runs for her life, stalked by a sadistic killer.

In a world where the Patriot Act has come to fruition, a man struggles to survive, despite eroding liberties.

Not able to accept his wife's death, a widower will cross into the dream realm to find her again, despite the dark forces that hold her in thrall.

These and other short stories will captivate and thrill you.

These are short stories to die for.

DEADFREEZE
By Anthony Giangregorio

THIS IS WHAT HELL WOULD BE LIKE IF IT FROZE OVER.

When an experimental serum for hypothermia goes horribly wrong, a small research station in the middle of Antarctica becomes overrun with an army of the frozen dead.

Now a small group of survivors must battle the arctic weather and a horde of frozen zombies as they make their way across the frozen plains of Antarctica to a neighboring research station.

What they don't realize is that they are being hunted by an entity whose sole reason for existing is vengeance; and it will find them wherever they run.

DEADFALL
By Anthony Giangregorio

It's Halloween in the small suburban town of Wakefield, Mass.

While parents take their children trick or treating and others throw costume parties, a swarm of meteorites enter the earth's atmosphere and crash to earth.

Inside are small parasitic worms, no larger than maggots.

The worms quickly infect the corpses at a local cemetery and so begins the rise of the undead.

The walking dead soon get the upper hand, with no one believing the truth.

That the dead now walk.

Will a small group of survivors live through the zombie apocalypse?

Or will they, too, succumb to the Deadfall.

ANOTHER EXCITING CHAPTER IN THE DEADWATER SERIES!

BOOK 5

DEAD HARVEST
By
Anthony Giangregorio

Lost at sea and fearing for their lives, a miracle arrives on the horizon, in the shape of a cruise ship, saving Henry Watson and his friends from a watery grave.

Enjoying the safety of the commandeered ship, Henry and his companions take a much needed rest and settle down for a life at sea, but after a devastating storm sends the companions adrift once again, they find themselves separated, exhausted, and washed ashore on the coast of California.

With each person believing the others in the group are dead; they fall into the middle of a feud between two neighboring towns, the companions now unknowingly battling against one another.
Needing to escape their newfound prisons, each one struggles to adapt to their new life, while the tableau of life continues around them.

But one sadistic ruler will seek to unleash the awesome power of the living dead on his unsuspecting adversaries, wiping the populace from the face of the earth, and in doing so, take Henry and his friends with them.

Though death looms around every corner, man's journey is far from over.

SEE HOW IT ALL BEGAN IN THE NEW
DOUBLE-SIZED EDITION!

DEADWATER: A Zombie Story
EXPANDED EDITION

By
Anthony Giangregorio

Through a series of tragic mishaps, a small town's water supply is contaminated with a deadly bacterium that transforms the town's population into flesh eating ghouls.

Without warning, Henry Watson finds himself thrown into a living hell where the living dead walk and want nothing more than to feed on the living.

Now Henry's trying to escape the undead town before he becomes the next victim.

With the military on one side, shooting civilians on sight, and a horde of bloodthirsty zombies on the other, Henry must try to battle his way to freedom.

With a small group of survivors, including a beautiful secretary and a wise-cracking janitor to aid him, the ragtag group will do their best to stay alive and escape the city codenamed: **Deadwater**.

ANOTHER EXCITING CHAPTER IN THE DEADWATER SERIES!
Book 3

DEAD CITY

By Anthony Giangregorio

NEW PERILS IN AN UNDEAD WORLD

After narrowly surviving an attack by a large pack of blood
thirsty, wild dogs, Henry and his companions stumble upon an
enclave that has made its home in an abandoned shopping mall.
Hoping for a respite from the perils of the walking dead, Henry
and the others plan to settle down for the winter, safe in the
company of fellow survivors of the zombie apocalypse.
But unknown to the group is the dark secret the enclave keeps, a
secret that could threaten to destroy the companions and anyone else unfortunate enough to be caught in the trap.
In a dead world the only thing still living... is hope.

DEAD END: A ZOMBIE NOVEL

By
Anthony Giangregorio

THE DEAD WALK!

Newspapers everywhere proclaim the dead have returned to
feast on the living!
A small group of survivors hole up in a cellar, afraid to brave the
masses of animated corpses, but when food runs out, they have
no choice but to venture out into a world gone mad.
What they will discover, however, is that the fall of civilization
has brought out the worst in their fellow man.
Cannibals, psychotic preachers and rapists are just some of the
atrocities they must face.
In a world turned upside down, it is life that has hit a Dead End.

THE NEXT EXCITING CHAPTER IN THE DEADWATER SERIES!

BOOK 7

DEAD VALLEY
by
Anthony Giangregorio

Untouched Majesty

After nearly drowning in the icy waters of the Colorado River, the six weary companions come upon a beautiful valley nestled in the mountains of Colorado, where the undead plague appears to have never happened.

With the mountains protecting the valley, the deadly rain never fell, and the valley is as untouched as the day it was created. But the group is soon captured by a secret, military research base now run by a few remaining scientists and soldiers.

On this base, unholy experiments are being carried out, and the group soon finds themselves caught in the middle of it. Mary, Sue, Raven and Cindy are taken away to be used as breeders, the scientists wanting to create a new utopia, which the living dead can't reach, but the side effect of this is the women will lose their lives.

Henry and Jimmy, now separated and captured themselves, must find a way to save them before it's too late; the scientists unleashing every conceivable mutation at their disposal to stop them.

In the world of the living dead, the past is gone and the future is non-existent.

LIVING DEAD PRESS

Where the Dead Walk

www.livingdeadpress.com

Book One of the *Undead World Trilogy*

BLOOD
OF THE
DEAD

A Shoot 'Em Up Zombie Novel by A.P. Fuchs

"*Blood of the Dead* . . . is the stuff of nightmares . . . with some unnerving and frightening action scenes that will have you on the edge of your seat."

- Rick Hautala
author of *The Wildman*

Joe Bailey prowls the Haven's streets, taking them back from the undead, each kill one step closer to reclaiming a life once stolen from him.

As the dead push into the Haven, he and a couple others are forced into the one place where folks fear to tread: the heart of the city, a place overrun with flesh-eating zombies.

Welcome to the end of all things.

**Ask for it at your local bookstore.
Also available from your favorite on-line retailer.**

ISBN-10   1-897217-80-3 / ISBN-13   978-1-897217-80-1

www.undeadworldtrilogy.com

DEAD WORLDS: Undead Stories
A Zombie Anthology

Edited by Anthony Giangregorio

Welcome to the world of the dead, where the laws of nature have been twisted, reality changed.

The Dead Walk!

Filled with established and promising new authors for the next generation of corpses, this anthology will leave you gasping for air as you go from one terror-filled story to another.

Like the decomposing meat of a freshly rotting carcass, this book will leave you breathless.

Don't say we didn't warn you.

www.ingramcontent.com/pod-product-compliance
Lightning Source LLC
Chambersburg PA
CBHW070948180726
48291CB00004B/1186